Samuel French Acting Edition

Glory

A hockey play that swings, by Tracey Power

SAMUEL FRENCH

FOR PRODUCTION INQUIRIES

UNITED STATES AND CANADA
info@concordtheatricals.com
1-866-979-0447

UNITED KINGDOM AND EUROPE
licensing@concordtheatricals.co.uk
020-7054-7200

Each title is subject to availability from Concord Theatricals Corp., depending upon country of performance. Please be aware that *GLORY* may not be licensed by Concord Theatricals Corp. in your territory. Professional and amateur producers should contact the nearest Concord Theatricals Corp. office or licensing partner to verify availability.

No one shall make any changes in this title(s) for the purpose of production. No part of this book may be reproduced, stored in a retrieval system, scanned, uploaded, or transmitted in any form, by any means, now known or yet to be invented, including mechanical, electronic, digital, photocopying, recording, videotaping, or otherwise, without the prior written permission of the publisher. No one shall share this title(s), or any part of this title(s), through any social media or file hosting websites.

For all inquiries regarding motion picture, television, online/digital and other media rights, please contact Concord Theatricals Corp.

MUSIC AND THIRD-PARTY MATERIALS USE NOTE

Licensees are solely responsible for obtaining formal written permission from copyright owners to use copyrighted music and/or other copyrighted third-party materials (e.g., artworks, logos) in the performance of this play and are strongly cautioned to do so. If no such permission is obtained by the licensee, then the licensee must use only original music and materials that the licensee owns and controls. Licensees are solely responsible and liable for clearances of all third-party copyrighted materials, including without limitation music, and shall indemnify the copyright owners of the play(s) and their licensing agent, Concord Theatricals Corp., against any costs, expenses, losses and liabilities arising from the use of such copyrighted third-party materials by licensees. For music, please contact the appropriate music licensing authority in your territory for the rights to any incidental music.

IMPORTANT BILLING AND CREDIT REQUIREMENTS

If you have obtained performance rights to this title, please refer to your licensing agreement for important billing and credit requirements.

GLORY premiered in 2018 as a co-production between Western Canada Theatre in Kamloops, British Columbia and Alberta Theatre Projects. The Western Canada Theatre production premiered on February 22, 2018, and the Alberta Theatre Projects production premiered on April 3, 2018. The productions were directed by James MacDonald, with choreography by Tracey Power, sound design by Steve Charles, set & lighting by Narda McCarroll, and costume design by Cindy Wiebe. The stage management team was Lisa Russel and Skylar Nazakawa. The cast was as follows:

HILDA RANSCOMBE	Katie Ryerson
NELLIE RANSCOMBE	Morgan Yamada
HELEN SCHMUCK	Kate Dion-Richard
MARGARET (MARM) SCHMUCK	Gili Roskis
HERB FACH	Kevin Corey

The national tour of *GLORY* was produced by Western Canada Theatre in 2019. The creative team was the same, and the show was stage managed by Jan Hodgson, Emma Hammond, Koh Lauren Quan, and Skylar Nazakawa. The cast was as follows:

HILDA RANSCOMBE	Katie Ryerson
NELLIE RANSCOMBE	Morgan Yamada
HELEN SCHMUCK	Kate Dion-Richard
MARGARET (MARM) SCHMUCK	Advah Soudack
HERB FACH	Andrew Wheeler

CHARACTERS

HILDA RANSCOMBE – 20-27
NELLIE RANSCOMBE – 22-29
HELEN SCHMUCK – 22-29
MARGARET (MARM) SCHMUCK – 20-27
HERB FACH – 40-50

SETTING

Even though the setting may change, the world of the play exists on the
ice of the Lowther Street Arena. The boards can be used to transition
from place to place.

TIME

1933-1939

AUTHOR'S NOTES

Choreography Notes

The hockey games are inspired by hockey technique and swing dancing. No skates of any kind are needed. The choreography should embrace the excitement of the game and what is happening in the story. Each game is different, expressing the demands of the story.

Sound Notes

The radio and the voice of the hockey announcer play an important role within the play. Electro Swing is the sound score of the play. A genre that incorporates music of the 1930s with a more modern drive and sound of modern day.

The announcers, umps, referees, and radio personalities are all live offstage voices or recorded voice-overs as in the original production. The game announcers are recorded over game music, and help the audience follow the action of the choreography. Using various voices for the announcers helps differentiate time and place for each game.

The text of CBC Radio and the announcer also help with scene transitions.

*In 1939, the penultimate note of "Oh Canada" went down, not up as we often hear it sung today.

Script Notes

A slash (/) signifies an overlap.

An ellipsis (...) signifies a character trailing off.

A dash (–) signifies a character being cut off or cutting themself off.

For the women who took to the ice and to the stage and inspired the next generation. Our bodies and our voices are stronger because of you. We must continue our fight for glory, against adversity, prejudice, and racism.

The Rivulettes were pioneers in the world of hockey. Along with many other women's teams, they fought to play a game they loved, a fight that continues today. This play was born from the many brilliant pieces of Rivulettes history. To the real-life Hilda and Nellie Ranscombe, Marm and Helen Schmuck, and Herb Fach,
thank you for being the inspiration for this play.

PROLOGUE

(An outdoor hockey rink. Music plays from a 1930s radio.*)

*(**HERB FACH** enters, water hose in hand. Light pours from the hose like water. While making ice, he looks around the rink, up into the stands, remembering when they were full. Remembering the team that last played there...his team.)*

(A 1930s-style pre-show announcement plays from the radio.)

---

*A license to produce *Glory* does not include a performance license for any third-party or copyrighted music. Licensees should create an original composition or use music in the public domain. For further information, please see Music and Third-Party Materials Use Note on page iii.

ACT I

Scene One
Just a Game

(A baseball diamond in Preston, Ontario, 1933. A high-energy song, circa 1933 with a driving beat, plays.*)

(The game is tense, the Rivulettes are down by one and up to bat in the bottom of the ninth. Dynamic bursts between runs and batters.)

(MARM SCHMUCK steps up to the plate. She looks to the outfield for any holes. She sets up and waits for the pitch. A lot of chatter can be heard from the WOMEN in the dugout.)

NELLIE. Here we go Marm! / Here we go!

HELEN. Nice and easy! / One little hit.

HILDA. Be patient up there.

    (MARM swings and misses.)

UMP. Strike one!

HELEN. Not your pitch Marmie! / Not your pitch!

HILDA. Wait for it!

    (MARM shakes it off and resets.)

---

*A license to produce *Glory* does not include a performance license for any third-party or copyrighted music. Licensees should create an original composition or use music in the public domain. For further information, please see Music and Third-Party Materials Use Note on page iii.

NELLIE. Watch it Marmie, she's knuckleballing it!

(*The pitch comes,* **MARM** *hits and runs. The cheering increases.*)

HILDA.   **NELLIE.**

  Nice hit!   There ya go Marmie!!

(*Rounding first,* **MARM** *heads to second.*)

HELEN. Go two Marm! / Go two, go two, go two!!

NELLIE. Run!!!! Ya, ya, ya, / ya, ya, ya, ya!

HILDA. Slide! / Slide! Slide!

(**MARM** *slides into second.*)

HELEN. Yes!

UMP. Safe at two.

NELLIE. More than safe! She's building a house on that bag!

HILDA. Careful.

(**HILDA RANSCOMBE** *walks up to the plate.*)

NELLIE. He gets up my knickers.

HELEN. Go get 'em Hill.

(**HILDA** *steps up to bat.*)

MARM. Hit me home, Hillbilly!

HELEN. My nerves!

NELLIE. We can do this girls!

HELEN. Why we always gotta save it for the ninth?!

NELLIE. Fifteen-fourteen girls! Let's tie this up!

HELEN. Make her pitch to ya!

NELLIE. Come on pitcher! Serve her a nice one!

(**HILDA** *sets up and waits for the pitch.*)

HELEN. Get ready to run, Marm!

NELLIE. Here we go Hill, here we go.

(**HILDA** *swings and hits. The ball goes foul.*)

UMP. Foul ball.

(**HILDA** *sets up again.*)

HELEN. Good contact!

NELLIE. You don't gotta rip the leather off it!

HELEN. Just straighten her out.

MARM. One little hit, Hillbilly. That's all we need.

NELLIE. She's gonna rip the leather off it.

(**HILDA** *hits the next pitch for a single. She runs to first.* **MARM** *runs to third.*)

HELEN.	**NELLIE.**
Nice hit Hill! Go third Marm, go third!	Go hard! Go hard! Run, run, run, YES!!!! Wooooo!!

(**HELEN SCHMUCK** *heads to the plate.*)

NELLIE. Go get 'em!

MARM. Let's tie this up right / now, Hells!

NELLIE. One little run.

(**HELEN** *steps up to bat.*)

HILDA.	**MARM.**
Here we go Helen!	Hit me home!

NELLIE. That's all we need. Just one little –

(**HELEN** *swings on the first pitch. A hit!*)

NELLIE. Nice! – Awe!

> (*They all start to run, but the ball is caught by the shortstop, and* **MARM** *and* **HILDA** *must get back quickly to their bags.*)

HELEN. Right to short!

UMP. Batter's out.

NELLIE.	**HELEN.**
Unbelievable!	You're kidding me!
HILDA.	**MARM.**
Nice try.	Unlucky.

HELEN. Straight to short!

UMP. Two away.

HELEN. Sorry.

NELLIE. Lucky catch.

> (**HELEN** *slaps* **NELLIE** *on the back as she heads to the plate, giving the field a look.*)

HELEN. You can do this!

NELLIE. (*Under her breath.*) Long and low. Long and low.

MARM. Take me home Nellie-pop!

> (**HELEN** *shoots* **MARM** *a look.*)

HILDA. Long and low! Where ya like 'em!

> (*The first pitch goes by.*)

UMP. Strike one.

> (**NELLIE** *looks at the* **UMP** *in disbelief.*)

NELLIE. Bit low.

HELEN. What? Are we lawn bowling now, ump?

MARM. Shake it off!

>   (**NELLIE** *steps back, then resets.*)

HILDA. Wait for it, Nellie. It's gotta be good.

MARM. No pressure, Nell. / No pressure.

HELEN. Come on, down the middle, pitcher!

>   (**NELLIE** *swings and hits.*)

Yes!! Run! Run!

>   *(It's a great hit, high into right field. The*
>   **WOMEN** *cheer loudly as they look to the sky.*
>   **MARM, HILDA,** *and* **NELLIE** *run home. They*
>   *all stand at home plate, anticipating the*
>   *victory...but the Port Dover outfielder catches*
>   *it.)*

ALL. *(Deflating.)* Uhhh.

NELLIE. No way.

RADIO ANNOUNCER. And there you have it! The Port
   Dover Sailorettes are the 1933 provincial champions!
   The Preston ladies losing to their rivals for the third
   year in a row!! The two teams pounded out hit after
   hit, but the Rivulettes strand the winning runs on base
   and fall to Port Dover fifteen-fourteen.

Scene Two
Now What...

(The locker room.)

MARM. Every year!

HELEN. I shoulda had it.

NELLIE. I popped that ball so high, she had time for a nap before she caught it.

HILDA. We were so close.

MARM. I hate Port Dover!

HELEN. Fifteen-fourteen!!

HILDA. It should've been over at the top of the fifth.

HELEN. So to come back like that?

MARM. Hilda pitched your butt out of hot water.

HELEN. What about yours?!

HILDA. Their pitcher's amazing.

NELLIE. Is her throw even legal?

HELEN. Are her legs? They don't even make stockings that long.

MARM. She's a gazelle!

HILDA. And she can hit. Two in-the-park home runs!

NELLIE. Just once I'd like to keep it on the ground.

MARM. The Nellie Pop is famous.

NELLIE. Can't I be famous for something else?

MARM. Imagine if she'd missed it! Ball to the head. Knocked out. We round the bases. Huge victory!

NELLIE. Wanna rub it in a little more?

MARM. I'm just saying, I liked your strategy.

HILDA. We'll get 'em next year.

NELLIE. We could play another month at least.

HELEN. It'll probably snow tomorrow.

MARM. What do you care?! You're off to university next week to make the rest of us look like uneducated nit twits.

> *(No one says anything...)*

What? ...What?

HELEN. *(To NELLIE.)* I didn't feel like it was my news to share.

NELLIE. It's nitwits, not nit twits and I'm not going.

MARM. Why?

NELLIE. Why do you think?

MARM. You put money aside!

NELLIE. Our dad's outta work.

HILDA. No one's buying houses.

NELLIE. Our brothers are still out west looking, so I'm the breadwinner in the family. Funny right?

MARM. No! It's depressing as shit.

HELEN. Everything's depressing as...to you.

MARM. They don't have quotas to worry about like we do.

HELEN. Marm, you can't blame –

MARM. If Nellie's last name was Schmuck she wouldn't even have the option. Sorry Nell, but if I were you, I'd say forget your family and just go.

HILDA. She can't just go.

MARM. *(To HILDA.)* Why don't you take her job?

HILDA. What?

MARM. You're her sister.

HILDA. ...

NELLIE. I'll go next year. I can survive sewing shoes for one more year.

MARM. I can't.

HELEN. You can too.

MARM. Fifty pairs a week for the next twelve months.

NELLIE. My fingers hurt just thinking about it.

HELEN. I'll be right there with you.

MARM. We gotta keep playing. I'll die of boredom in there if we don't.

HILDA. It's that bad?

MARM. Fifty pairs a week!

HELEN. I'm not playing softball in the snow.

HILDA. What if we –

HELEN. We could curl!

(The WOMEN groan.)

There's four of us! We could start a curling team!

MARM. Forget it.

NELLIE. You'd make the rest of us look bad.

HELEN. I love curling!

MARM. Kill me now.

NELLIE. Curling with you, would be like playing hockey with Hilda.

HILDA. We could / start –

MARM. I can play hockey!

NELLIE. Not like Hilda you can't.

MARM. How do you know?

NELLIE. 'Cause when she shows up on the river, the boys pick her first.

HELEN. Is that true?

HILDA. Someone's gotta pick the girl.

NELLIE. Not first they don't.

HILDA. I didn't used to get picked at all.

NELLIE. They'd make her watch. Then one day they were playing so badly, she jumped on the ice, stole the puck, raced toward the net, and scored.

> *(They all look at* **HILDA***.)*

HILDA. I was so nervous I peed my pants.

NELLIE. It's legendary.

HILDA. Not the peeing –

NELLIE. The playing.

HILDA. I've always wanted to play on a team.

> *(They all look to one another, not sure what to say.)*

MARM. Let's do it then!

NELLIE. I'm not playing hockey.

HILDA. Please, Nellie.

MARM. You both know how to skate.

NELLIE. Not like Hilda!

HILDA. We practice.

HELEN. I didn't even know girls played hockey. Are there teams?

NELLIE.	HILDA.
Hardly.	Yes.

NELLIE. Preston doesn't have one.

MARM. We start one!

HELEN. Who would we play?

HILDA. Port Dover has a team.

HELEN & MARM. We hate Port Dover!

NELLIE. The Gazelle on ice?

MARM. Revenge, Nellie!

HILDA. There's the London Silverwoods. Stratford Aces. Charlottetown Islanders. Toronto has a couple of teams. So does Montreal. Ottawa. Winnipeg. There's even teams out west. Vancouver, Calgary.

HELEN. How do you know all this?

HILDA. *(A little embarrassed.)* "The No Man's Land of Sports."

MARM. Huh?

HILDA. The column in the *Star*.

NELLIE. She won't read the news, but the sports!

HELEN. I don't know, Hillbilly. Hockey seems a bit –

HILDA. It's the best game in the world. I'll teach you. I'll –

> **(FACH** *enters, but doesn't come directly into the locker room.)*

FACH. Hey! Out in five minutes!

MARM. Mr. Fach! Come in here... What if I told you the Rivulettes are gonna play hockey?

FACH. What do you mean?

HILDA. A ladies hockey team.

FACH. ...

MARM. It's a hockey team... With girls on it.

FACH. Girls don't play hockey.

HILDA. Some do.

FACH. *(Amused.) You* wanna play hockey?

NELLIE. We're a joke and we haven't even played a game.

MARM. It's not a joke, Mr. Fach.

FACH. You sure about that? A bunch of dolls tossin' a puck around.

>*(Laughs.)*

...I dare ya.

>*(**FACH** leaves... A moment...)*

NELLIE. I'm in!

HELEN. Me too.

NELLIE. But you've gotta help me.

HELEN. And me!

NELLIE. And I'm not playing goal.

MARM. We need to join a league.

HILDA. Alexandrine Gibb's in town! Covering the ball game for the paper. She knows everything about women's sports.

MARM. Do you think she'd talk to us?

HELEN. What about uniforms? We'll freeze our cupcakes off in those.

NELLIE. We don't have any money.

HILDA. There's a bunch of old gear at the arena.

HELEN. The boys' team might have some old uniforms we can spruce up.

NELLIE. Have you smelled one of those things?

HILDA. I'll ask George to have a look.

MARM. Ooo, Georgey.

NELLIE. There's gotta be fees, travel, equipment.

HILDA. Karl Homuth supports the boys' club.

MARM. Who?

NELLIE. Karl Homuth. The guy with the huge cowlick.

HELEN. Our MLA.

MARM. That guy's our MLA?

NELLIE. He actually gets his head licked by a real live cow.

HILDA. If he supports the boys then –

MARM. He can support us.

HELEN. Worth a try.

NELLIE. We can change our name to the Preston Cowlickers.

I'll talk to the other girls and see who's in.

MARM. Toddy and Myrtle will play.

HELEN. And Violet! Violet's a great skater.

HILDA. What about a coach! Who can we get to coach?

(They leave.)

Scene Three
Coach or Dare

RADIO ANNOUNCER. As we come up on the three-year anniversary of the crash of the New York Stock Exchange, we await the Aird Commission's recommendation for a nationally owned company, the CRBC, to operate a coast-to-coast broadcast system. In international news...

> (**FACH** *enters, holding a water hose, making ice, with* **HILDA** *in tow. They talk over the radio, until* **FACH** *becomes distracted by what he hears.*)

BBC ANNOUNCER. *(Translating over part of the original Rudolf Hess speech from February 25, 1934.)* German men, German women, German boys, German girls. Over a million of you are gathered in many places in all of Germany!

FACH. A coach? What do you need a coach for?

HILDA. We joined the league.

FACH. Who did?

HILDA. The Rivulettes.

FACH. ...A *ladies'* hockey league

HILDA. Miss Gibb said – She's the sports writer for the *Toronto Star*. The *women's* sports writer. She said women's hockey is really starting to take off, which is –

FACH. Hold on.

> (**FACH** *turns up the radio.*)

BBC ANNOUNCER. On this the anniversary of the proclamation of the party's program. You will together swear an oath of loyalty and obedience to Adolf Hitler.

(**FACH** *turns the radio off and goes back to making ice.*)

HILDA. Uhh...Bobbie Rosenfeld is the head of the Ladies' Ontario Hockey Association. I talked to her. Can you believe it? I talked to Bobbie Rosenfeld!

FACH. Who?

HILDA. She said the association demands that we all be local. Local ladies, local coach.

FACH. You want me.

HILDA. Yes.

FACH. To coach a *ladies'* hockey team.

HILDA. Oh! You don't need to be a... Other – non-ladies are coaching as well.

FACH. Ladies shouldn't play hockey.

HILDA. Karl Homuth thinks we'd be good for civic morale.

FACH. Karl likes to hear himself talk.

HILDA. He's investing in the team.

FACH. It's part of his job.

HILDA. If you agree to coach us.

FACH. Pardon me?!

HILDA. We went to talk to him. He said you played together. When you were kids. You were on the same team.

FACH. I don't play anymore.

HILDA. He thinks you'd be a good coach –

FACH. – Of a ladies' hockey club?

HILDA. That's what he said.

FACH. I'm not coaching you.

HILDA. But...we need you to.

FACH. Find somebody else.

HILDA. He's only investing if –

FACH. I don't know what *ladies* need to play hockey!

HILDA. A stick and a puck.

FACH. What rules they play with!

HILDA. The same as the men.

(**HELEN, MARM,** *and* **NELLIE** *burst in.*)

MARM. And we don't wear dresses or lipstick when we play either.

HELEN. We don't?

NELLIE. But sometimes I might bring my laundry so I can iron between periods.

MARM. Nellie! You said period.

FACH. What's this?

NELLIE. Half the team. Violet, Myrtle, Margaret and Toddy are in too.

FACH. Eight of you? That's it?

HILDA. Mr. Homuth's giving us the season to prove we can compete.

MARM. And if we're good, he'll reinvest.

FACH. This is hockey. It's a men's game.

HILDA. It's a National game.

NELLIE. Women make up half –

FACH. Doesn't matter! When you think of hockey, you think of men. When you go to a game, there's men playing. I'm not doubting your athletic abilities.

HELEN. I think you are.

FACH. Do you really want to subject yourself to that kind of...? It's not like softball, it's aggressive, it's –

MARM. We might break a toenail.

FACH. You'll break a hell of a lot more than that. And who wants to watch that? A bunch of... No one's going to NHL games right now! You think the people of Preston are gonna dig into their empty pockets and watch you?

MARM. We just wanna play! We don't need people to watch!

FACH. Course you do, else you can't afford to play. That's how it works. The money from the gate pays for the travel, the equipment, the first-aid kits – which I guarantee you're going to need, the ice-time if the men's league will spare you any.

HILDA. Maybe people can't afford the dollar it costs to watch the Leafs. But I bet they can afford the twenty-five cents to watch us.

FACH. Twenty-five cents is a lot to some people.

MARM. It's four cans of beans.

FACH. Which is a lot to some people!

HELEN. Without the money –

HILDA. We can't afford to play.

NELLIE. I gave up going to university, I'm not giving up sports as well.

MARM. All you have to do is let us in the arena.

HELEN. You don't have to talk to us.

NELLIE. You're here anyway. Just unlock the door so we can practice.

HILDA. Please, Mr. Fach.

MARM. I dare ya.

(A long pause.)

FACH. Tomorrow. Six a.m.

HELEN. Six a.m.?!

Scene Four
Practice Makes...

*(The **WOMEN** skate onto the ice, each grabbing sticks from behind the boards. **FACH** leans on the boards, reading the* Prestonian, *the local newspaper.)*

NELLIE. Is he gonna stand there the entire practice?

HILDA. Looks like it.

MARM. Apparently, he and his family –

HELEN. Marm!

MARM. – Were interned during the war.

HELEN. Dad told us that in confidence!

MARM. Nellie and Hilda should know. In case anything happens.

HELEN. What's going to happen?

MARM. He's German isn't he?

HELEN. It was fifteen years ago! If he was guilty of something he wouldn't be here right now.

MARM. I think it's good that we're all aware –

HELEN. No, it's not, and you should've kept your mouth shut. Hilda?

HILDA. Everyone fine holding a stick?

HELEN. No.

HILDA. Let's see.

HELEN. ...

MARM. You look uncomfortable.

HELEN. I wonder why?!

HILDA. ...Pretend it's a curling broom, but hold it to the side. Like... Here. Stick your bum out. Not so much... It should feel like it's a part of your body. Then when the puck comes, your blade is on the ice and –

> (**HILDA** *makes a pass.* **HELEN** *attempts to make a pass.*)

HELEN. It doesn't feel like a part of my body.

HILDA. It will.

HELEN. In two months?

HILDA. We don't need to be perfect. We just need to know how to poke the puck in the net.

FACH. Your opponent's net.

HILDA. The better we can skate, pass, and shoot, the better the chance of that happening.

FACH. *(Snorts.)* Hrrg.

> (*The* **WOMEN** *look to* **FACH.** *He's still behind the newspaper.*)

HILDA. Ready position. The stance. Uh...

(Demonstrating.) Knees bent...like you're about to run. Then use your edges to push off and slide. Push off and slide.

FACH. Glide.

HILDA. Dig in hard for speed. Push off and slide.

FACH. Glide.

MARM. What's he saying?

FACH. The proper term is glide. Slide gives the impression that you're not in control. Which, under the circumstances might be the case.

HILDA. I'm trying to –

FACH. You're teaching the wrong terms. You wanna make a fool of me in the press *and* on the ice?!

> (**FACH** *holds up the paper, and the headline on the front page of the sports section reads, "Herb Fach, is one of the girls."*)

NELLIE. Herb Fach, is one of the girls.

HILDA. We didn't do that.

FACH. Your new friend Karl did. Women's hockey'll be good for civic morale? Was he laughing when he said that?

> (*Beat.*)

Four basic skills of hockey: skating, stick-handling, passing, shooting.

HILDA. What are you doing?

FACH. Saving what little reputation I have left, Miss Ranscombe. Let's see your stance! Knees bent. Legs strong. Ready? ...Ready?!

NELLIE.	**MARM.**
Yes.	I'm ready.
HILDA.	**HELEN.**
Ready.	Yes.

FACH. Now skate!

> (*The music kicks in.* * *The movements establish a basic choreographic vocabulary for the games. Each of them is at a different skill and ability level.*)

---

*A license to produce *Glory* does not include a performance license for any third-party or copyrighted music. Licensees should create an original composition or use music in the public domain. For further information, please see Music and Third-Party Materials Use Note on page iii.

Push, GLIDE. Push, GLIDE. Push, GLIDE. Push, GLIDE. Push, GLIDE. And...stop. STOP!

> *(**NELLIE** slips and falls.)*

NELLIE. Slipped.

HILDA. Use your edges and –

FACH. Again! Ready?! Now skate! Push. Glide. Push. Glide. Now, cross over to the left. Watch Miss Ranscombe.

> *(They look to **NELLIE**, whose legs have slipped away from her. She's bent over with her bum in the air.)*

No! The one who knows what she's doing.

> *(They look to **HILDA**.)*

Cross over right. And...stop. STOP!

> *(**NELLIE** slips, spins in a circle, and falls.)*

NELLIE. There's a really slippery patch right –

FACH. Line up! Ready? Now skate! Push, glide. Push, glide. Push, glide, and...turn!

HELEN. Turn?

FACH. Around!

> *(**HELEN** does a pirouette.)*

Not – This isn't ballet Miss Schmuck. Turn around and go the other way!

HELEN. Why didn't you just say so?

> *(**HELEN** coyly turns and skates back to the group.)*

FACH. Stick-handling.

*(**HILDA** stick-handles, and the other **WOMEN** follow suit.)*

FACH. Keep your heads up. Look around. You want to keep the puck in front of you. On the back half of your blade. Move the puck back and forth. Back and forth. Shoulders relaxed. Keep 'em down Miss Schmuck.

MARM. What?

FACH. No! The other Miss Schmuck. Shoulders relaxed. Back and forth. Back and forth. Relaxed, Miss Schmuck!

HELEN. *(Her shoulders are up at her ears.)* I'm sorry.

FACH. Don't apologize.

HELEN. I'm sorry.

FACH. Stop! You gonna apologize every time you take someone into the boards? Every time you score and the goalie looks like they're gonna cry?

HELEN. If it'll make her feel better.

FACH. Passing.

(They set up, each facing a partner.)

Puck on your stick. Eyes on your target, ideally who the puck's going to, and push the puck. Ready? Push the puck.

(See them pass the puck.)

Follow through. And again.

(They pass the puck again.)

Eyes on the target. Push the –

(And again.)

MARM. I see myself as more of a scorer.

FACH. Really.

MARM. I'm in front of the net! Hilda pass me the puck!

FACH. No one likes a cherry picker, Miss Schmuck! Learn to pass.

Shots. Concentrate on the backhand, wrist and snap shot.

HILDA. And the slap shot.

FACH. I don't think so.

HILDA. You get the most power. Like hitting a softball but on ice. Eddie Marten uses it, he plays for the colored hockey league.

FACH. Well, no one's using it in the NHL. It's unreliable.

HILDA. Unless we can perfect it, then it's deadly.

FACH. Alright, Miss Ranscombe. Line up. Let's go. Let's go! Miss Ranscombe, stand in front so they can watch.

> (**HILDA** *demonstrates once, and then the others join.*)

Backhand. Wrist. Snap.

HILDA. And slap.

FACH. Backhand. Wrist. Snap.

HILDA. And slap.

FACH. Backhand. Wrist. Snap.

WOMEN. And slap.

FACH. And back to stance. Ready? Skate! Push. Glide. Push. Glide. Cross over left...and STOP!

> (**NELLIE** *slips and flies into the boards.*)

There's your goalie.

NELLIE. What? No. You can't put me in net.

(**FACH** *grabs a pair of goalie pads and tosses them to* **NELLIE**.)

FACH. You'll lose. You'll blame yourself. You'll get over it.

NELLIE. No, I can't –

FACH. Whether it's your fault or not, you'll get over it. That's your job.

(**FACH** *hands her a goalie stick.*)

NELLIE. But I'm –

HILDA. I'll play goal.

FACH. No.

HILDA. I –

FACH. *(To* **NELLIE**.*)* You wanna make a difference on this team? Do you?

NELLIE. Yes.

FACH. Do it in net. Let your sister score the goals. See the puck. Get in its way. That's all ya gotta do. The team needs a captain.

HILDA. We don't –

FACH. Hilda, that's you. Get some newspaper in those socks, save your shins. There's not enough of you to afford getting hurt. Tomorrow, you can have the ice when the men are done. Eleven p.m.

HELEN. Eleven p.m.? I work at seven the next morning.

FACH. Then it doesn't conflict. You wanna play hockey, ladies? Then man up!

(*They watch* **FACH** *leave.*)

MARM. I thought he was just unlocking the door...

Scene Five
Manning Up

RADIO ANNOUNCER. Unemployment has reached a record high of twenty-seven percent across the country. One look at the food line at the Yonge Street Mission in Toronto will tell you, we've got a lot to bounce back from. The Depression's like a disease, folks. It spreads and even those of you, who are lucky enough to have jobs, will feel its effect.

> *(On the Grand River.* **NELLIE** *and* **HILDA** *take off their sweaters to make goalposts.)*

HILDA. Actually, you have the perfect mental strength to be a goalie. You're focused. You're patient. And you hate to lose almost as much as I do.

NELLIE. See the puck. Get in its way.

HILDA. Ready?

> *(***HILDA** *takes a shot.)*

NELLIE. *(Dodges a puck to the face.)* Ah!

HILDA. Sorry.

NELLIE. A blind goalie?

HILDA. I'll shoot lower.

> *(She takes a tiny shot, and* **NELLIE** *stops it.)*

Good save!

NELLIE. You shot it right at my stick.

HILDA. Five mornings a week. Two months. You'll be stopping more shots than Tiny Thompson.

NELLIE. Tiny is exactly how I'm feeling right now.

HILDA. I still can't believe I talked to Bobbie Rosenfeld! She's the superwoman of women's hockey, Nell! What

I wouldn't give... And she's from Barrie! Which makes anything seem possible!

NELLIE. Hill, I gotta talk to you about something. They cut our wages at the factory this week.

HILDA. What?

NELLIE. In half!

HILDA. They can do that?

NELLIE. What are we gonna do, quit? It's making me nervous. The line at the soupy's around the block. Remember Henry Adams?

HILDA. His family owns the garage on the corner.

NELLIE. He came to the door this morning looking for food. To our home. These are people we know.

HILDA. *(Hopeful protest.)* Dad went to the office today.

NELLIE. To sit and pray that someone comes in. No one's coming in.

HILDA. They will. Everyone needs a place to live.

NELLIE. Not if they can't afford it. You have to start thinking about finding a job for yourself.

HILDA. Ready for some higher ones?

NELLIE. They'll need a girl at the factory soon. Sarah's having a baby. You should talk to them.

HILDA. George needs a job.

NELLIE. It's cheaper to hire a woman.

HILDA. Pay him a woman's wage. He won't care.

NELLIE. Hill, if you don't get a job now, you won't get one.

(Getting hit on the elbow.) Ow!

HILDA. Sorry.

NELLIE. Right on my...

HILDA. If Bobbie Rosenfeld can make a career for herself playing sports, then why can't I?

NELLIE. She also worked in a chocolate factory. Did you forget that part?

HILDA. I don't know how to sew.

NELLIE. Then sell.

(Grabs her boob.) Ah!

HILDA. Nice save!

NELLIE. I'm gonna have an inside-out nipple!

HILDA. Newspaper?

NELLIE. What about my face?

HILDA. Sorry, I'm not smarter.

NELLIE. Would you stop?! If you had as much confidence at school as you do on the ice, you'd be smarter than all of us put together.

HILDA. You could wear a mask to protect your face. Clint Benedict wore a leather one when he broke his nose.

NELLIE. Are you kidding? I gotta "man up" remember.

Scene Six
The First Game

ANNOUNCER. Good afternoon hockey fans, and welcome to the Grimsby Arena, where your hometown hockey honeys will be taking on the newest addition to the Ontario Ladies' Hockey League, the Preston Rivulettes.

(MARM and HELEN warm up on the ice.)

HELEN. I don't want you to be disappointed.

MARM. It's just a letter, Helen. I bet Annie Epstein had the same problem as me when she was applying for schools.

HELEN. Maybe.

MARM. I got a ninety-percent average.

HELEN. I know that.

MARM. There's kids getting in with sixty and I'm pickin' shoe glue outta my nails while the university decides whether or not to let another Jew in.

HELEN. Mail it then.

MARM. I have to do something.

HELEN. Just don't expect –

(Seeing the other team.) Oh my gosh!

MARM. Wow. They look –

HELEN. Like they know what they're doing? Look at her arms! They're bigger than my thighs!

MARM. Farm girls.

HELEN. Your body adapts to the sport, I read it in *Chatelaine*, it becomes more athletic.

MARM. What's wrong with that?

HELEN. The article asked fifty men whether they prefer a woman who had a more athletic figure like...or a more feminine one like... *(She refers to herself.)*

MARM. I don't care what fifty men in *Chatelaine* think!

HELEN. Guess which one they picked?! I don't want my muscles bulging out of my blouse like that.

MARM. You're not serious?

HELEN. I'm gonna get killed out there! Do you think they can tell I'm a curler?

MARM. ...Untuck your shirt.

> *(**HELEN** untucks her shirt.)*

Mess up your hair a bit.

> *(**HELEN** thinks about it and then untucks her shirt some more.)*

> *(**HILDA** rushes in with **NELLIE**.)*

HILDA. Girls! We have to win this game.

HELEN. Did you see the other team?!

MARM. They've really manned up.

HILDA. It's the playoffs.

MARM. What playoffs?

HILDA. Ours.

HELEN, NELLIE & MARM. What?!

HILDA. I think, I was a bit nervous when I talked to Bobbie Rosenfeld, and I forgot that – she did say something about entering the season late, meant that we'd be starting during the playoffs.

MARM. You forgot?

HILDA. If we don't win this, we're done.

HELEN. I've never played a game before!

NELLIE. I've never been a goalie before!

MARM. Fine! Let's just – What's the name of the other team?

(**FACH** *from behind the boards:*)

FACH. The "Grimsby Peaches."

WOMEN. Peach farmers?!

NELLIE. I feel nauseous.

HILDA. Gather in, gather in.

(*They all rush over to* **FACH.**)

FACH. ...What?

HILDA. The coach always says something to the team before a game.

HELEN. Especially when it's about to be their last.

FACH. ...It's your first game... Don't expect too much.

MARM. That's it?

NELLIE. I'm going out there to get shot at!

FACH. By a Peach.

HELEN. Hilda, you say something.

HILDA. Me?

NELLIE. I have an inside-out nipple because of you!

HILDA. Uh – It's our first game. And – So – That's what they'll be thinking. They, uh... They think we're an easy win. That it's going to take us the whole game just to figure out how to play. But – we know how to play. We've practiced – at ridiculous hours. In outrageously cold temperatures – so we know how to move to keep warm. Let's use our speed ladies! And put that puck in the net before they do.

(Whistle: To the ice.)

NELLIE. Oh no.

(The Rivulettes vs. The Peaches.)

(The **WOMEN** *skate out.* **MARM** *at center.* **HELEN** *on left wing.* **HILDA** *on right wing.* **NELLIE** *in goal.* **FACH** *stands behind the boards, reading his paper.)*

(Whistle and Game One music: * *The game is adrenaline-filled. Klutzy at first, struggling to find rhythm.)*

(The dialogue in Game One, as in all the games, often overlaps with the **ANNOUNCER.***)*

ANNOUNCER. Marm Schmuck wins the face-off.

HILDA. Marm! Marm!

ANNOUNCER. A swift pass to Ranscombe.

MARM. Hey!!

ANNOUNCER. That's broken up by the Peaches defense. It's up ice to Blake.

HILDA.	**HELEN.**
Get back! Get back!	This way! This way!

ANNOUNCER. Who skates in on the Rivulettes' goaltender, / a wrister from Blake.

NELLIE. Get it outta here! Get it outta here!

(Glove save by **NELLIE.***)*

ANNOUNCER. Quick save by Ranscombe.

---

*A license to produce *Glory* does not include a performance license for any third-party or copyrighted music. Licensees should create an original composition or use music in the public domain. For further information, please see Music and Third-Party Materials Use Note on page iii.

(Whistle: Stop play.)

NELLIE. It's in my glove! It's in my glove!!

HILDA. Marm, take the face-off.

MARM. Where?

HILDA. Where the ref is!

(Whistle: Game back on.)

ANNOUNCER. Grimsby wins the face-off.

HELEN. *(Hip check.)* Hah!

ANNOUNCER. Ooo, what a hit by Schmuck.

HELEN. Oh my gosh! I just hit her!

ANNOUNCER. We've got two sets of sisters on this team folks. We might need to get on a first-name basis here. Marm Schmuck now with the puck. Not sure what to do with it.

HELEN. Marm! Pass!

ANNOUNCER. A quick pass to her sister, to Ranscombe, to Schmuck, to Schmuck, to Schmuck again, to Ranscombe –

NELLIE. Someone shoot it already!!

ANNOUNCER. – To Marm Schmuck, who takes a shot and that's wide.

MARM. Get in there!

ANNOUNCER. The pressure is all in the Peaches' end.

NELLIE. Shoot! Just keep shooting!

ANNOUNCER. The Rivulettes, bombarding the Grimsby goaltender.

NELLIE. Please somebody get it in the net! Please!

ANNOUNCER. Webb to Schmuck – *SCORES!*

(Whistle: **MARM** *scores.)*

NELLIE. Yes!!!!

MARM. It went in. Did you see that?! It! Went! In!

>   (**HILDA** *and* **HELEN** *swoop in and they celebrate.)*

ANNOUNCER. Marm Schmuck, with the first goal of the hockey game! The first goal ever for the Rivulettes!

HELEN.   **HILDA.**
That was so good!!   Nice shot Marm!

NELLIE. I feel really far away back here.

>   *(Whistle: Game on.)*

One more would be good! One more would definitely be good!

ANNOUNCER. It's Hilda Ranscombe on the breakaway. Impressive speed from the winger, very impressive, wrist shot. *SCORES!*

>   *(Whistle:* **HILDA** *scores.)*

HILDA. *(Frozen to the spot, so happy she could cry.)* I scored?

ANNOUNCER. Hilda Ranscombe!

HILDA. I scored!

HELEN.   **MARM.**
Nice goal Hillbilly!!   Two-nothing!

NELLIE. *(Waving her stick in the air.)* I'm really far away back here!

>   *(Whistle: Game back on.)*

HELEN. How long do we play for?

MARM. Don't say that out loud!

ANNOUNCER. Ten minutes into the second period and the Rivulettes are still up two-zero. Here come the Peaches.

HILDA. Get back!

ANNOUNCER. Look at Hilda Ranscombe. I've never seen a girl skate that fast!

NELLIE. Get it out of here, Hilda!!

ANNOUNCER. It's a two-on-one headed toward the Rivulettes' net.

NELLIE. Get it out of here!

ANNOUNCER. Ferris shoots.

NELLIE. No!!

> *(Whistle: Grimsby scores.)*

ANNOUNCER. *SCORES!* Nellie Ranscombe has seen her first miss here in Grimsby. Surprise! You will get scored on sweetheart.

> *(**HILDA** skates over to **NELLIE**, who's a little shook up.)*

HILDA. It's just one.

> *(Whistle: Game back on.)*

NELLIE. See the puck, get in its way. See the puck, get in its –

ANNOUNCER. The Peaches need more action in that end if they want to make a game out of it. The Rivulettes are not easing up. Marm Schmuck with the puck.

HELEN. Over here!

ANNOUNCER. Schmuck. To Schmuck. To Schmuck. To Webb. To Schmuck. To Ranscombe. A slap shot? *SCORES!!*

> *(Whistle: **HILDA** scores. Game over.)*

HILDA. Yes!!!!

> (*The* **WOMEN** *pile on* **HILDA** *in celebration.*)

ANNOUNCER. That goal seals the deal. A three-one victory for the Rivulettes and they're off to the semifinals!

Scene Seven
The Taste of Blood

(MARM, NELLIE, HILDA, *and* HELEN *in the locker room.*)

NELLIE. She came straight for me!

MARM. My lungs are bleeding!

NELLIE. Didn't even try to stop!

HELEN. She slammed her elbow right under my ribs!

NELLIE. Then she drilled the puck straight at my neck!

MARM. I can taste blood!

NELLIE. She coulda decapitated me!

MARM. I'm serious, I can taste blood!

HELEN. It's adrenaline.

MARM. That tastes like blood?!

NELLIE. Terrifying!

MARM. Three-one?!

HELEN. How'd we do that?

MARM. We're not even very good yet!

(*They jump around screaming in celebration and then notice* HILDA *sitting quietly on the bench.*)

NELLIE. Hill? ...Hillbilly you okay?

HILDA. ...I've never felt anything so good in my entire life. I was flying down the ice. Marm passed me the puck – I saw the net. I don't even remember shooting. I just saw the puck go in.

MARM. We're one for one!

(They all cheer.)

HILDA. We have to prove this team belongs here. That we –

*(**FACH** walks into the locker room.)*

WOMEN. AHHHHHH!

*(The **WOMEN** scream and cover up, even though they haven't undressed.)*

FACH. *(Realizing where he is.)* Right, you're uhhh... Good!

*(**FACH** quickly leaves. The **WOMEN** all look at each other and then burst out laughing.)*

Scene Eight
I Hate Port Dover

(**HILDA** *is in the locker room. She pulls a dress
out of her bag and tosses it on the bench and
proudly looks at her jersey.*)

ANNOUNCER. Next up folks, it's the *ladies'*, that's right,
you did hear me correctly, the *ladies'* semifinal matchup
between the Preston Riv-ulettes, I think that's how you
say that, and the Port Dover Sailorettes. Port Dover are
last year's Ontario Champions, so the newby Rivulettes
are going to be in for a hard-fought battle!

(**HELEN** *rushes in.*)

HELEN. The Gazelle's already skating around, marking
her territory, stretching her legs out another couple of
inches.

HILDA. If Port Dover's as tough on the ice as they are
on the field we're in big trouble. Of all the teams we
coulda... We just started!

HELEN. *(Going for the dress.)* You remembered!

HILDA. We can't lose yet!

HELEN. Hold it up.

HILDA. Right now?

HELEN. Is it for a date?

HILDA. Not one that costs money.

HELEN. He's still outta work?

HILDA. If George can't find a job, who can? I've been
thinking about it all week. I've never wanted something
so badly in my whole life. I can see it. Our future. What
we could be, and...

HELEN. George is a big boy. He'll figure it out.

HILDA. Not George! The team!

HELEN. Oh, well…

HILDA. Hockey comes first for him too you know. Who do you think taught me how to shoot?

HELEN. I'm sure he'd like to teach you a lot more than that.

HILDA. What if Mr. Homuth stops supporting the team?

HELEN. Don't think like that.

HILDA. If we could get enough fans buying tickets to our games, we wouldn't need his support.

HELEN. Fat chance! Our own coach isn't even a fan. I might have some lace I could add along the seam here.

HILDA. Sounds fancy.

HELEN. Fancy's not a bad thing. You can't be Hillbilly forever!

HILDA. Everything in my closet's starting to fall apart.

HELEN. We'll all be wearing rags together.

HILDA. Don't you think people would enjoy watching us play just as much as the boys?

(**MARM** *enters.*)

MARM. Did you see their uniforms?!

HELEN. They are the *Sailorettes*.

MARM. Well, I'm not buying their "too cute to cross-check you" routine.

HELEN. It is a little fishy.

HILDA. If our games can be as good – as competitive as the boys, then it shouldn't matter.

MARM. What shouldn't matter?

HILDA. That we're girls.

(NELLIE enters.)

NELLIE. If I throw up on the ice, just haul me off.

MARM. Nervous, Nellie?

NELLIE. Don't you mean Nellie-Pop? Port Dover? Are we actually doing this?

MARM. Revenge?

(From outside the locker room:)

FACH. Let's go ladies! We're starting right now!

HILDA. We still got half an hour.

FACH. The ice time's double-booked. The men need to practice.

HELEN. We have a game to play!

FACH. You got an hour.

WOMEN. What?! / An hour!

HILDA.	**MARM.**
We need more than –	It's the semifinal!

NELLIE. It's Port Dover!

FACH. You wanna play or not?! Let's go!! Let's go!!

(Rivulettes vs. Sailorettes.)

(Music: Game Two.*)

ANNOUNCER. If you can take your seats folks. Looks like we're gonna get started early here so we can give our boys their ice back. Those Sailorettes, sure know how to wear a uniform. There's nothing wrong with ladies' hockey when you look like that.

---

*A license to produce *Glory* does not include a performance license for any third-party or copyrighted music. Licensees should create an original composition or use music in the public domain. For further information, please see Music and Third-Party Materials Use Note on page iii.

*(Whistle: The game is choppy and aggressive.
A definite feel of frustration and holding it
together against a better team.)*

(The **WOMEN** *jump into the action.* **FACH**
stands behind the boards.)

And there they are folks! Look at 'em go. No one ever
said playing hockey was gonna be easy for the dainty
ones among us. If nothing else, it'll be entertaining!

HELEN. *(Takes a hit from the Gazelle.)* Agh!

ANNOUNCER. Ouch! Helen Schmuck is down on the ice.
That's gotta hurt.

HILDA. Hey ref, aren't ya gonna call that?

ANNOUNCER. I wouldn't want someone hittin' my girl like
that.

HILDA. Hey ref!

FACH. Play the whistle, Miss Ranscombe!

ANNOUNCER. Port Dover, rushing the Rivulettes' net.
Look at the legs on number –

NELLIE. *(Getting bumped out of her net.)* Ah!!

ANNOUNCER. Nellie Ranscombe bumped hard out of her
net by Harris!

NELLIE. Damn it!! She's not allowed to do that!

ANNOUNCER. Sweeps the rebound to her sister. Who
sends it up ice to –

MARM. *(Her head snaps back and she grabs her mouth.)*
Uhh!

ANNOUNCER. Whoa! A high stick to the mouth of Marm
Schmuck.

HILDA. You're not gonna call that, ref?!

ANNOUNCER. She'll wanna pull out the makeup kit
tomorrow.

MARM. Shit!!

(Whistle: Intermission.)

(They all gather at the boards. FACH *tosses* MARM *a towel.)*

HILDA. What's going on out there?!

FACH. Leave it, Miss Ranscombe.

MARM. I got a mouth full of blood!

HILDA. If the ref doesn't start calling those hits, I'm gonna start hittin' him.

HELEN. The Gazelle's using me as a punching bag!

NELLIE. They're all over us!

FACH. Let him do his job. You do yours.

HILDA. He's not doing his job, that's the problem.

FACH. You're lucky he stuck around.

HILDA. What do you mean?

FACH. He thought he was reffing a men's game.

(They all turn to look at the ref.)

I told you, it's –

MARM. We heard you.

NELLIE. Look at him.

MARM. He does not wanna be here.

HELEN. He wasn't good enough to make the local team, and then to top it all off his penis never grew!

NELLIE. Makes sense!

HILDA. Just put the puck in the net. He has to call that.

(Whistle: Game on.)

(The Rivulettes are peppering the Port Dover net with shots.)

ANNOUNCER. Another shot from Ranscombe, her tenth of the period. Look at her go! From the point. Slap shot?! *SCORES!*

(Whistle: **HILDA** *scores.)*

Wow! Your brother show ya how to do that?!

HILDA. See that, ref?!

FACH. Let it go, Miss Ranscombe!

ANNOUNCER. The Rivulettes lead one-zero.

(Whistle: Game on.)

It's Helen Schmuck with the puck now!

HELEN. *(Taking the Gazelle into the board.)* Huh! Get offa me!!

ANNOUNCER. What a hit by Helen Schmuck! Collins sent flying! To Ranscombe, who holds on to it, takes it behind the net, jams it in the side – *SCORES!*

(Whistle: **HILDA** *scores.)*

A perfect wraparound goal from the little lady!

HILDA. *(To the ref.)* Didn't think a little lady could do that, did ya ref?!

FACH. Alright, Miss Ranscombe, just get it out of your system.

HILDA. I've had a pair of skates on from the time I could walk. I don't wanna get it out of my system!

(Whistle: Game on.)

ANNOUNCER. Collins for the Sailorettes, racing back to pick up Schmuck.

(**HELEN** *is off after Collins, the Gazelle.*)

ANNOUNCER. Schmuck, eyeing her up. This much tension in women's hockey! Is that healthy?

HELEN. *(Cross-checking the Gazelle.)* You, bitch!

ANNOUNCER. Whoa! Helen Schmuck lays out – Ladies don't hit like that! Do they? They allow men in this league?

HELEN. What?!

ANNOUNCER. Schmuck to Ranscombe back to Schmuck – Snap shot! *SCORES!*

(*Whistle:* **HELEN** *scores. Game over.*)

(*The* **WOMEN** *celebrate their victory.*)

The Rivulettes with the win! Collins still down on the ice! Helen Shmuck, with a – There's no way! Come on, she's gotta be a man!

HELEN. *(Hearing the* **ANNOUNCER.***)* Hey!! Do I look like a man to you?!

(**HELEN** *flashes the* **ANNOUNCER.***)*

NELLIE. Helen!

(**NELLIE** *skates over to shield* **HELEN.***)*

FACH. What the hell was that?! Captain! One of your players just flashed her –

NELLIE. *(Thinking she's hilarious.)* Wah-wahs?

MARM. *(Likewise.)* Cannons!

FACH. – To an arena full of people.

HILDA. It was her brassiere. Technically.

HELEN. He accused me of being a man!

FACH. It's not appropriate Miss Schmuck!

MARM. You said we needed fans.

FACH. That's not how you get them.

HELEN. He had no right to say that.

FACH. He could've said a lot worse.

MARM. Like, look at the little Jewish girls trying to play hockey.

HELEN. Does everything have to be a joke with you?!

MARM. Sorry, one Jewish girl, one Jew-*ish* –

FACH. You humiliated yourselves out there!

HILDA. We just beat Port Dover! Who cares if she –

FACH. I do! What kind of ladies are you?!

MARM. I don't feel comfortable with you yelling at me or my sister like that.

FACH. You don't?

MARM. It's not *appropriate*.

HILDA. Because we're girls, a ref doesn't have to do his job? The announcer can say whatever he wants about the way we look, the way we play. We're trying to be the best *players* on that ice. Not the best *girls*. If I can think like that, why can't they, why can't you?

FACH. Because I'm not used to seeing girls smash one another into the boards like that. Seeing blood fly out of their faces. Cursin' at one another.

MARM. You said man up!

FACH. It ain't...right!

   *(**FACH** leaves... Silence.)*

HILDA. I guess we've got more to win than just games.

HELEN. I don't know who that was out there. It wasn't decent.

MARM. We beat Port Dover!

HELEN. Flashing my breasts didn't help us do that! I shouldn't have let him get to me.

NELLIE. No one's gonna take what we're doing seriously until they have a reason to. Even then. People think the money Mr. Homuth gave us should've gone to charity.

HILDA. Well, they're wrong. If people need a reason to take us seriously...let's give them one.

(They head off the ice.)

Scene Nine
Mind on the Game

ANNOUNCER. Welcome! To the Belleville Arena in Pembroke, host of your Provincial Ladies' Hockey Finals. The Preston Rivulettes and the Pembroke Ladies are just entering the arena now, having entertained the local fans with a parade down Main Street! Neither team's been in a final before so you can imagine the nerves on these little ladies.

(**HELEN** *and* **NELLIE** *are in the locker room.*)

NELLIE. I didn't know there was a right pad and a left pad. Not until Fach told me. I've been wearing them on the wrong legs this entire time. They look exactly the same! We won the first two games with me wearing my pads on the wrong legs but I can't change them now! If we lose, it'll be because I didn't play with them on the legs I had them on be–

HELEN. Nellie! You're making *me* nervous now!

NELLIE. I'm just going to wear them on the wrong legs.

HELEN. Good idea.

NELLIE. They're the right legs to me! This is *not* getting any easier.

(**NELLIE** *sits next to* **HELEN**, *and* **HELEN** *takes her hand.*)

HELEN. You've only let in one goal!

NELLIE. And it felt awful! I'm not saving goals out there; I'm trying to avoid throwing up!

(**MARM** *enters.*)

MARM. We should ride in a parade before every game. I feel famous or something.

(*Coyly looking at* **HELEN**.) Uh-oh...

NELLIE. I made her nervous.

MARM. Was it you? Or was it Mr. Willys Whippet saying, "I'll be watching."

HELEN. Marm!

NELLIE. Who's Mr. Whippet?

MARM. Her driver in the parade. He was driving a shiny red Willys Whippet. Helen can't resist a man with a set of hot pistons.

HELEN. Shut it, Marm!

NELLIE. It's just a car.

MARM. It's not the car she liked. It's the driver.

HELEN. He's got front-row seats!

MARM. Practically sitting on the ice.

HELEN. Okay!

MARM. My driver was a seventy-year-old cattle farmer, with a Ford. He's watching too but he's not having the same effect.

NELLIE. *(To* **HELEN.***)* Really?

HELEN. He's never seen a girl play hockey before.

MARM. If you lift your shirt up again –

HELEN. Marm!

NELLIE. We're doing this for us, not him.

MARM. Not anymore.

HELEN. Look at me! What's he gonna think?!

NELLIE. Who cares?!

> *(Silence.* **HILDA** *enters.)*

HILDA. Let's get out there Ladies! What's the holdup?

> *(Feeling the silence.)* What happened?

NELLIE. Mr. Willys Whippet is watching.

HELEN. Nellie.

HILDA. Who?

MARM. *(Mimes that her mouth is shut.)* ...

HILDA. We're playing for the provincial title remember?! Let's go!

(The Rivulettes vs. The Pembroke Ladies.)

ANNOUNCER. Things are getting tense here in Pembroke. This ain't no NHL but you've gotta admire their commitment. Oh, haha, would ya look at that! The coach for the Rivulettes might wanna tell his netminder she's wearing her pads on the wrong legs. A puck slippin' through a right pad would be a lousy way to lose a final.

(Music: Game Three.* The **PLAYERS** *scramble to play together. Their focus is split. Tension grows between* **HELEN** *and* **NELLIE,** *and* **HILDA** *doesn't understand why.)*

Nellie Ranscombe with the puck now. Passes the puck to Helen Schmuck, who can't get her stick on it.

FACH. Let's get some focus out there!

ANNOUNCER. Looking scattered in their own end. Pembroke with the steal.

NELLIE. Get back! Get back!

ANNOUNCER. Ranscombe caught out of her net – *SCORES!*

(Whistle: Pembroke scores.)

---

*A license to produce *Glory* does not include a performance license for any third-party or copyrighted music. Licensees should create an original composition or use music in the public domain. For further information, please see Music and Third-Party Materials Use Note on page iii.

NELLIE. I passed it right to you!

HELEN. You did not!

HILDA. Are you alright?

NELLIE. I'm fine.

(*Whistle: Face-off.*)

ANNOUNCER. Helen Schmuck wins the face-off.

NELLIE. Helen!!

MARM. Too far!

ANNOUNCER. Ooo! A bad pass to her sister results in a steal by Downs who drills the puck up the ice.

NELLIE. Marm! I need help back here!

FACH. You're fine Ranscombe.

ANNOUNCER. A scramble in the Rivulettes' end.

MARM. Hilda!

ANNOUNCER. Marm Schmuck passes to Hilda Ranscombe, who carries it into the Pembroke end.

NELLIE. Come on.

ANNOUNCER. Crosses to Helen Schmuck

NELLIE. Come on!

ANNOUNCER. To Margaret Schmuck

NELLIE. Come on!!

ANNOUNCER. Back to her sister, shoots! Nice save!

NELLIE. And again!

ANNOUNCER. Rebound. *SCORES!*

(*Whistle:* **HELEN** *scores.*)

NELLIE. Finally!

MARM. Willys Whippet makin' you nervous too, Nellie?

(Whistle: Game back on.)

ANNOUNCER. Pembroke shoots! Save by Ranscombe.

NELLIE. Clear it!!

ANNOUNCER. Georgia Downs with the rebound – Another save by Ranscombe.

NELLIE. Clear it, Helen!

ANNOUNCER. Helen Schmuck trying to clear the puck. The warm weather making for unruly ice conditions.

HELEN. Where is it?!

ANNOUNCER. Helen Schmuck slashing through the slush now –

NELLIE. Watch it!

ANNOUNCER. Georgia Downs with the steal. Shoots!

NELLIE. Ah!!

ANNOUNCER. *SCORES!* It's two-one Pembroke.

(Whistle: Pembroke scores.)

HELEN. Sorry!

NELLIE. Uhh.

*(**NELLIE** runs to the boards.)*

HELEN. The ice is melting!

NELLIE. *(Throws up.)* Hulllllll.

HILDA. Nellie!

HELEN.	**MARM.**
Oh my gosh.	Oh no.

FACH. What's wrong with her?!

NELLIE. I quit.

FACH. You can quit in twenty minutes.

NELLIE. I'm quitting now!

HILDA. It's the finals!

NELLIE. I don't care.

HILDA. We can't play without a goalie?!

NELLIE. *(To* **HELEN.***)* What were you doing?!

HELEN. It's like ice soup!

HILDA. We've gotta get back in this!

NELLIE. *(Going to* **HELEN.***)* Get your mind on the game!

HELEN. *(Pushing her away.)* Excuse me?! You're the one –

HILDA. *(Pulling them apart.)* Stop it!!

MARM. Smarten up!

HILDA. We need to be a team right now or we've lost this!

MARM. It's the provincial final!

HILDA. Let's go!!

> *(Whistle: Game back on.)*

ANNOUNCER. The Rivulettes' top line need to pick up their skates if they want to get this game back. Marm Schmuck passes back to her goalie, to Ranscombe, to Helen Schmuck; takes a quick shot.

> *(Whistle:* **HELEN** *scores.)*

SCORES!! Helen Schmuck has tied the game!

HELEN. *(Skating over to* **NELLIE.***)* Not my fault you cleared the puck into a puddle.

NELLIE. Not my fault boys with shiny cars make you nervous!

> *(Whistle: Game back on.)*

ANNOUNCER. Toddy Webb on defense for the Rivulettes skates up ice, leaves the puck for Helen Schmuck

FACH. See Hilda!

HELEN. Hill!

ANNOUNCER. Five seconds on the clock. Schmuck, passes it off to Ranscombe on the rush, *SCORES!!* A beautiful pass from Helen Schmuck and Hilda Ranscombe gives the Preston Rivulettes the provincial title. What a story for these ladies.

> *(Whistle:* **HILDA** *scores.)*

FACH. *(Clapping for the first time.)* Good job, boys! Girls – Ladies.

> *(The* **WOMEN** *jump around in a mass celebration.* **NELLIE** *and* **HELEN** *don't know how to respond to one another.)*

Ladies?! They wanna take your picture.

MARM. Get over here Nell! I need your big shoulders! Hilda's are too boney!

> *(***MARM** *climbs on* **NELLIE***'s shoulders with* **HELEN** *and* **HILDA** *on either side. They smile for the camera)*

(Smelling her jersey.) Ugh, I stink!

HILDA. Let's get changed.

> *(***MARM** *and* **HILDA** *head to get changed.* **HELEN** *stops* **NELLIE** *before she heads off too.)*

HELEN. What was that about?

NELLIE. What?

HELEN. You know what?

NELLIE. I thought you wanted...

HELEN. What? ...Tell me.

NELLIE. It's fine... I'll see you at work.

>*(**NELLIE** heads off. **HELEN** watches her leave...*
>***FACH** walks onto the ice and takes **HELEN** by*
>*surprise.)*

FACH. You turned it around today Ms. Schmuck. Good end to the season.

HELEN. We were just getting started.

FACH. Men's league, the Eastern champs play the Western champs. Can't see it happening with the ladies though.

HELEN. Not yet.

>*(**HELEN** skates off.)*

>*(**FACH** picks up a stick that's been left on the ice. He steps onto the ice, looks up into the stands. He grabs a puck that was left along the boards. He brings it over to center ice, lines up the puck, winds up, about to take a shot...but he stops himself.)*

>*(He pushes the puck to the side of the ice and tosses the stick on top of the net.)*

Scene Ten
From There to Here

(At the Wragge Shoe Company, **NELLIE,** **MARM,** *and* **HELEN** *huddle around the radio.)*

RADIO ANNOUNCER. And another local hockey season has come to an end. But this year it was the remarkable performance of the local girls' team that caused considerable comment among sports fans. Leaving many confused by the sudden feminine desire to compete at our country's greatest game. But why shouldn't girls get a shot at the puck? Organized as a team only a short time ago, inexperienced and unnoticed, the Rivulettes made their way with ease through all their opposition, to bring the ladies' championship honor home to Preston. So, who are we to decide hockey's only for the boys. Whatever your view, they've got us wondering, where will the little hockey dolls go from here?

MARM. *(Mimicking.)* "Where will the little hockey dolls go from here?"

NELLIE. *(Looking around the shop.)* The Wragge Shoe Company, that's where.

MARM. Fifty pairs a week!! I've gots the depression!

NELLIE. Time to polish up the ol' Nellie Pop. Or maybe I'll aim for the dirt this summer.

HELEN. Listen to this!

(From a magazine.) "There are sports of which women are physically and temperamentally unfit. Ice hockey is a game, for which their soft, yielding flesh is unsuited."

MARM. No.

HELEN. "The spectacle of pretty girls losing their tempers in a rink, and watching dimpled fists and tufts of hair fly all about, is not a sight I enjoy. Not that the girls didn't put plenty of zip into the job –

NELLIE. Zip?

HELEN. – They surely did! Yet, I wouldn't care to see them in the prize ring, either. I may be funny about my women that way, but there it is."

MARM. Thankfully, we're not *his* women.

HELEN. Why would a women's magazine print something so unsupportive.

MARM. Athletic maidens to arms! Any man, or woman! Who doesn't see me as a model of feminine physique, can go to hell.

NELLIE. Our perfect thirty-sixes may be ruined!

MARM. Our features may become "Frankensteinish"!

HELEN. I'm hangin' on to my femininity no matter how hard I hit some girl into the boards.

MARM. I won't be satisfied until I'm considered more than just the hockey playing "rib of Adam."

HELEN. Write that down! Send it to the magazine.

NELLIE. I should!

MARM. Forget being a school teacher, you can be a – I don't know what you'd call it, a teacher of –

HELEN. The new feminine! It's sweaty. It's bruised.

MARM. And it has muscles that aren't afraid to bulge.

HELEN. A little bulge.

NELLIE. Instructing from the pages of *Chatelaine Magazine*?

MARM. Exactly! So instead of reading this crap, we'd read about how girls aren't afraid to knock the teeth outta Port Dover.

HELEN. Fat chance! Miss Chatelaine just told me I'm unfit to play hockey, not because of my talent, because of my vagina!

MARM. Ohhh! The big V.

NELLIE. What did Mr. Willys Whippet think?

MARM. Of her big V?

NELLIE. Of her playing hockey!

HELEN. I'm taking your advice and trying not to care.

NELLIE. Really?

HELEN. Really. If it wasn't for hockey he'd never have met me.

MARM. Well, he's got a bigger battle to win on the whole *not being Jewish* front.

HELEN. It's not important.

MARM. What? …You think Mom and Dad would agree with that?

HELEN. Would you just be happy for me?!

MARM. Bubbie would roll over in her grave.

HELEN. I'm not going to marry someone just because they're Jewish. If Whippet's the one, and I haven't said that he is, then they'll have to get over it.

NELLIE. *(Sincerely.)* Well, it's good to know he doesn't mind a girl with a stick in her hand.

MARM. Most guys don't.

NELLIE. I meant – That's not what I meant.

> (**HILDA** *rushes in, holding a letter in her hand.*)

HILDA. Girls!! There's going to be a Dominion title!

OTHERS. What?

HILDA. The Eastern Champs against the Western Champs!

HELEN. You're kidding?!

HILDA. The first ever!!

HILDA. *(Enthusiastically trying to read.)* Officially invited, you're – And a trophy! We compete for the – A real trophy. The Lady Bessborogh trophy!

MARM. Lady who?

HILDA. She donated it. The governor general's wife.

HELEN. What?! When? *Where?!*

NELLIE. Here?

HILDA. In Edmonton.

MARM. Edmonton?

NELLIE. Alberta?

HELEN. How far is that?

NELLIE. Far.

HILDA. To play the Rustlers.

MARM. The Rustlers?! A team of cow-stealers?

HELEN. Girls in Edmonton do that?!

NELLIE. How much will it cost?

HILDA. 1,500 dollars.

NELLIE.	**HELEN.**
Wow!	1,500 dollars!

MARM. We're not going.

HILDA. But they're paying.

NELLIE. They have 1,500 dollars?

MARM. Do they steal the cows, then sell them?

HELEN. That's a lot of stolen cows.

HILDA. If we win this? We'll be the National Champions.

MARM. Holy shit!

NELLIE. The best in Canada.

MARM. Don't you think? That really is, holy shit!

HELEN. *(Tossing the magazine down.)* Hear that Miss Chatelaine?!

NELLIE. And Fach agreed to go?

HILDA. Yes.

MARM. Alone on a train with Fach?

HELEN. I can't tell if you're serious.

HILDA. We'll have chaperones with us.

MARM. He's not exactly rooting for us.

NELLIE. He's coming around.

MARM. I don't trust him.

HELEN. Don't stir it up, Marm.

MARM. He was interned for a crime!

HELEN. You'll keep on this until you've dug up a whole rack of crap.

MARM. Why would Mr. Homuth, suggest he coach our team when he doesn't play?

HILDA. He used to.

MARM. He won't even pick up a stick. We're like a perverse form of community service.

HILDA. We need him. People are really starting to believe in us. If we win the Dominion title, Mr. Homuth will *have* to support us!

HELEN. So drop it.

MARM. ...Fine! ...But it's weird.

NELLIE. *This* is weird! A group of *hockey dolls* traveling 2,000 miles for a hockey game?! It doesn't get much weirder!

Scene Eleven
A Date With a Cow Stealer

(FACH enters, weighed down with suitcases, hockey sticks, and goalie pads. He squeezes himself and the gear onto the train.)

CRBC RADIO ANNOUNCER. The ladies wave goodbye to fans as they board the train bound for their greatest adventure yet. Putting our little town of Preston on the map as they face the Edmonton Rustlers. Hard to believe our hometown hockey heroes are of the female variety. We'll wait, with bated breath, to hear how our lovely queens of the ice lanes fare this time.

(The WOMEN wave goodbye to fans from the platform, then board the train and wave a final farewell from the train.)

HILDA. That's a lot of people.

MARM. You think they're gonna throw rocks at us if we lose?

HILDA. Would they?

MARM. Hillbilly!! No team from Preston's ever gone across the country for a hockey game.

HILDA. George was so jealous when I said we were going.

MARM. The guys' team stinks this year! I guess it's not their fault. Half their players left lookin' for work.

(MARM and HILDA settle side by side.)

HILDA. Bobbie Rosenfeld says pressure's what separates good athletes from great ones. How they deal with it.

MARM. If you knew you were this good, why didn't we do this sooner?

HILDA. I didn't know we could. I'd read about women's teams, but I'd never actually seen one.

MARM. You can't hold yourself back, Hillbilly.

(Pulls a letter out of her purse.)

See this. Annie Epstein wrote me back.

HILDA. Who's that?

MARM. A lawyer. A Jewish lawyer. The first female one in Canada. I wanna be the second.

HILDA. You wanna be a lawyer?

MARM. Helen's always telling me to stop stirring it up, but that's what lawyers do. I know I'd be good if they'd just let me in.

HILDA. Are you still on the list?

MARM. Yeah, but I gotta find a way around it. Annie said I could come volunteer for her, learn the ropes in Montreal.

HILDA. You can't leave the team.

MARM. I'd go in the summer.

HILDA. I know we're not professional, but – ...Or maybe...

MARM. What?

HILDA. You think they'd ever let women play in the NHL?

MARM. We're as fast as they are. You can shoot the puck better than most of them.

HILDA. I don't wanna job I'm not good at.

MARM. Then don't Hillbilly. Be the next Bobbie Rosenfeld. Jewish by the way!

HILDA. She had to work in a chocolate factory.

MARM. Then be better than Bobbie Rosenfeld.

*(Times goes by... **HELEN** looks out the window,
and **NELLIE** comes and sits down next to her.)*

NELLIE. Can't sleep?

HELEN. *(Shakes her head.)* Mm-mm.

NELLIE. Me neither... Feels like we're running away.

HELEN. I know. Can you imagine? Some sleepy little seaside town where nobody knows us.

NELLIE. New life. New jobs.

HELEN. Preston hockey dolls on the lam.

NELLIE. When I think of what my brothers did, going out west for work, taking a chance like that... We could go too... If we wanted.

HELEN. ...

NELLIE. Maybe not right now but –

HELEN. Nell, do you like Whippet?

NELLIE. I don't know him, Hells.

HELEN. He wants to marry me.

NELLIE. ...Congratulations.

(Times goes by...)

MARM. Haaachuu!!

HILDA. You're not getting sick are you?

MARM. The woman in the back hasn't stopped blowing her nose for two days.

HELEN. I don't want to get it.

NELLIE. Don't think about it.

MARM. Feel this? The Gazelle gave me a bald spot.

HILDA. She gave me three stitches.

HELEN. Not an ounce of femininity left in that woman.

HILDA. I'd still take a win with a few stitches over a loss.

NELLIE. You'd take a win with stitches, a broken arm and five missing teeth.

HILDA. George told me, he saw a skate blade fly off its boot and stick right into a man's stomach.

HELEN. Uh! I'm never playing again.

MARM. How many teeth do you think you can get knocked out before your whole face caves in?

NELLIE. More than one. Let me see.

>   (**NELLIE** *looks in* **MARM***'s mouth.*)

MARM. When I stick my tongue in it, it feels like a massive pit.

NELLIE. You have a big tongue.

MARM. It's just fat. It's short and fat. I can barely stick it out. See... Let me see yours.

>   (**NELLIE** *sticks her tongue out.*)

Look how long it is! Look at that! You're probably a good kisser.

NELLIE. You think?

MARM. Kiss me and I'll tell you.

FACH. Good grief. I can hear you, ya know.

MARM. Cheese and Rice! Where are we? It's flatter than my chest out there!

>   (**FACH** *stands up from a back seat.*)

FACH. Saskatchewan. Didn't you see the sign? "Welcome to Saskatchewan. Flatter than Margaret Schmuck's chest."

(Nobody laughs...)

HELEN. I think he just made a joke.

HILDA. I think it was slightly inappropriate.

FACH. It was. Excuse me.

MARM. You look a bit trapped back there, Fach.

FACH. Yeah.

MARM. What kind of name is Fach anyway?

*(**HELEN** shoots **MARM** a look.)*

FACH. ...German.

MARM. I thought it might be, so, do you know a man by the name of...oh, what's his name again...Adolf Hitler?

HELEN. *(Mouths.)* Stop it.

FACH. Not personally. No.

MARM. Hmm, and what does Fach mean exactly? German for...?

FACH. Pocket.

MARM. Pocket? ...You're Mr. Pocket? ...Coach Pocket?

FACH. This from a girl named, Schmuck.

MARM. It's actually pronounced Shmewk but it's funnier when people get it wrong.

FACH. Well, mine's pronounced Fuck, it's funnier when people get it right.

*(The **WOMEN** can't help but laugh.)*

NELLIE. *(Running to the window.)* Look!

FACH. The prairies are getting hit the worst. The drought didn't help either.

HELEN. Geez, it looks –

MARM. A ghost town.

NELLIE. 1,500 dollars to play a hockey game when half the country is starving. Don't you feel guilty?

FACH. People need it. The best part of a person's day might be catching a game on the radio.

MARM. Even if it's only, *ladies'* hockey...

FACH. Even if.

HELEN. Coach Pocket might be one of the girls after all.

FACH. Alright.

NELLIE. A little time in the ladies' locker room will do that to ya.

FACH. Alright.

HELEN. So, how long until we get to Edmonton?

FACH. Eight hours.

HILDA. And when's game time?

FACH. ...Eight hours.

Scene Twelve
The Dominion Championship

(In the locker room, the **WOMEN** *rush to get ready.)*

CRBC RADIO ANNOUNCER. Hello Hockey Fans, and welcome to the first ever National Women's Dominion Championship! 2,500 fans are here tonight to witness the first ever matchup between our local Western Champions, the Edmonton Rustlers, and the Eastern Champions, the Preston Rivulettes. Women's hockey is producing high-caliber players in the east and west, with skills and speed matching some of our top men. One of those players we welcome to our fair city is Hilda Ranscombe!

MARM. What am I chopped gizzards?

HELEN. Hilda's the top scorer.

HILDA. The whole team's the top scorer. We play together. We win together.

FACH. Hurry up ladies!

HELEN. We're going as fast as we can!

HILDA. Can't you just tell the ref there was a moose on the tracks?

FACH. No. Just hurry up.

NELLIE. What kind of excuse is that?

MARM. That's what the conductor said! The train was late –

NELLIE. 'Cause there was a moose on the tracks?!

HILDA. Was it alive?

MARM. Before we hit it!

HELEN. Oh no!

MARM. What do you think happened?

HELEN. I thought it was just standing there eating something.

HILDA. It probably was.

MARM. Before we killed it!

FACH. Step on it ladies!!

HILDA. Ahh-choo!

HELEN. Don't think about it.

FACH. Some guy named Clarence Campbell's reffing. He's local. So play clean.

HILDA. What are you saying?

FACH. Local's local. Don't give him any excuse to blow his whistle.

NELLIE. Ahh-choo!

MARM. Damn that lady!

HELEN. Don't think about it!!

HILDA. Listen up. Today we're playing for the honor of being the best women's hockey team in Canada...and we're not going home to tell our fans we lost to a bunch of cow-stealers.

MARM. If they weren't depressed before, they will be then.

HILDA. Let's go! Let's go! Let's go!!

> *(They rush onto the ice and gather around* **FACH.***)*

FACH. Alright ladies! Three days on a train... Let's make it count.

NELLIE. You have a way with words, Coach.

ALL . *(Hitting the ice with their sticks.)* Riiiiii-vulettes!!

(The Rivulettes vs. The Edmonton Rustlers.)

(Whistle: Game on. Hardworking. The team is very focused, the most in sync we've seen them. **FACH** *gets more and more into the game as it progresses.)*

ANNOUNCER. It's Marm Schmuck winning the face-off for the Rivulettes but she can't hold on to the puck and it's Muriel Tufford for Edmonton moving fast.

FACH. Let's go ladies.

ANNOUNCER. Choppy play from both teams off the top here. The Rivulettes not able to keep hold of the puck.

FACH. Find some control out there.

ANNOUNCER. Tufford picks it up, to Duncan, back to Tufford.

FACH. Get back! Get back!

ANNOUNCER. To Duncan, to Tufford, shoots.

(Whistle: Rustlers score.)

SCORES! The first shot of the game and the Edmonton Rustlers are up one nothing in the first.

FACH. They're not gonna just give it to you, ya gotta fight for it.

(Whistle: Game back on.)

ANNOUNCER. The Rivulettes trying to gain control. Ranscombe takes a shot. Great save by Hoffman, for the Rustlers.

FACH. Get on that!

ANNOUNCER. Schmuck with the rebound! No! She can't get it past Hoffman.

MARM. *(Getting hit.)* Uh!

FACH. The defense is all over you!

HELEN. *(Getting hit.)* Uh!

ANNOUNCER. Helen Schmuck bobbles the puck and Duncan with the steal heads up ice on the breakaway. Duncan's in all alone.

FACH. Come on! Come on! Get back!

> *(Whistle: Rustlers score.)*

ANNOUNCER. *SCORES!* Cheryl Duncan puts Edmonton up two-zero at the end of the first.

> *(First intermission: The* **WOMEN** *skate to the bench.)*

HILDA. We're panicking! / We need to settle it down.

FACH. You need to settle the puck down.

NELLIE. They're shooting high!

FACH. Get your body in front of it.

HILDA. Nellie was wide open!

HELEN. I can't catch my breath.

FACH. Just, calm down. You're –

HELEN. There's no room out there!

FACH. They're shooting on everything. / You need to do the same.

HILDA. We should be using / the corners more.

FACH. Ranscombe! Can I coach now?! ...You're scrambling out there. Nellie's bailing you out all over the place. You'd be down ten-nothing if it wasn't for her. Come on, you gotta focus. You control the play. Make *them* scramble. You fought to get here, now fight to win.

> *(Whistle: Game back on. Period two. Determined and recharged by Fach's words.)*

ANNOUNCER. The Rivulettes have found their legs in the second. Now, this is the team we've heard about! Look at that speed. Nice stick work by Schmuck, to Ranscombe, to Schmuck, to Ranscombe. Shoots. *SCORES!*

(Whistle: **HILDA** *scores.)*

HILDA. Yes!! One more!!

FACH. There we go! Nice work, ladies! Short, crisp, passes! One more! Let's even this up!

(Whistle: Game picks up.)

ANNOUNCER. The game has sped up here in the second. The Preston goalie, coming up big on some end-to-end rushes by the Rustlers.

FACH. Go, go!

ANNOUNCER. Marm Schmuck with the steal from Duncan.

FACH. There ya go!

ANNOUNCER. Pass to Ranscombe – Two on one! Helen Schmuck! *SCORES!* And we're tied at two...

(Whistle: **HELEN** *scores.)*

FACH. There ya are!!

(The **WOMEN** *skate over to the bench.)*

Good work, ladies! It's a new game now.

HELEN. I can't breathe.

FACH. Sit. Take a break.

MARM. My head feels like it weighs fifty pounds.

FACH. Don't think about it.

NELLIE. I feel like I've been sittin' on my butt all day.

FACH. You can't back down.

HILDA. Three days.

FACH. You gotta keep the pressure on them.

> *(Whistle: Game back on. Period three. The game is wearing on the players, but they're fighting hard.)*

ANNOUNCER. Still tied at two here in the dying moments of the third period.

FACH. You can do this! Dig deep!

HILDA. *(Getting hit.)* Uh!

ANNOUNCER. Ooh! Ranscombe taken to the ice!

FACH. What was that?!

HELEN. *(Getting hit.)* Ow!

ANNOUNCER. Helen Schmuck is down.

FACH. Hey! Let's see some calls, ref!

ANNOUNCER. Ooo, that is a nasty split lip.

NELLIE. *(Making a save.)* Out!

ANNOUNCER. Nellie Ranscombe coming up big again in net.

FACH. Nice save, Miss Ranscombe!

HILDA. Marm!!

ANNOUNCER. Schmuck to Ranscombe –

MARM. *(Getting hit.)* Awe!

ANNOUNCER. Ooo, Marm Schmuck getting hit hard.

FACH. What was that?! A little more attention, ref! They too quick for ya! There ya go Ranscombe! You're all alone! It's all yours!

> **(HILDA** *on the breakaway.)*

ANNOUNCER.

A breakaway for Ranscombe! / Racing down the ice – This could be it! She's all alone!

FACH.

Shooot!!

Ohhhh!!

FACH.

Skate, Ranscombe, skate! You got time! You got – Shoot!!

ANNOUNCER.

She shoots! OHHH!!

HILDA.

No!!

ANNOUNCER. Misses the net! What an opportunity! Now it's Duncan back the other way!

FACH. GET BACK!

NELLIE. Get back!!

HILDA. GET BACK! / GET BACK!

FACH. GET BACK!

ANNOUNCER. Schmuck can't stop Duncan at the line.

HILDA. Go! / Go! Go!

FACH. Get in front of her!

ANNOUNCER. Splits the defense, to Tufford.

FACH. Get in front of her!

ANNOUNCER. Shoots! *SCORES!!!!* And the game is over!

> *(Whistle: Rustlers score.)*

> *(The **WOMEN** collapse in utter disappointment. They watch the other team celebrate. There's nothing to say.)*

It's Murial Tufford for the Rustlers! With a beautiful goal!! A disappointing end for the Rivulettes but what a battle! So there they are folks, the first ever Canadian Ladies' Hockey Champions! Your EDMONTON RUSTLERS!

(Silence except for the sound of breathing and sobs. **FACH** *climbs over the boards.)*

FACH. You played hard ladies... You did... You played a good game, it just... It just wasn't your time to win.

HILDA. ...I had it.

FACH. Next year.

HELEN. There might not be a next year.

HILDA. The game was on my stick.

FACH. ...That's the glory of sport. You can be up one second, and down the next. Anything can happen. That's what makes us wanna play. That's what makes them wanna watch... They found a way to win today ladies. But next time...

*(***HILDA*** *stands.)*

HILDA. We will.

ACT II

Scene Thirteen
Staying Afloat: 1938

(A spotlight comes up on the four **PLAYERS***, standing in a tight group.)*

WOMEN. *(In three-part harmony.)*
THE BOYS CAN PULL OFF GIFTED PLAYS
THEY SCINTILLATE AND STAR;
BUT WHERE YOU SEE THE THOUSANDS GAZE –
THAT'S WHERE THE GIRLS' TEAMS ARE

THE BOYS CAN PLAY A PERFECT GAME
AND ERR WE WOULDN'T BET
BUT STILL THE FANS SHOUT OUT OUR NAME
PRESTON "SPRINGS" RIVULETTES

MARM. *(To* **FACH.***)* Was that good enough?

> *(The lights open up; the team jumps into a photo shoot. Posing for the cameras uncomfortably as the announcement plays. Their shirts now read "Preston Springs Rivulettes."* **FACH** *sits watching from the bench.)*

RADIO ANNOUNCER. Thanks to our friends at the Preston Springs Hotel, our girls are sittin' pretty. They've come a long way, folks. If you call a record of 250 wins a long way! You're lucky to find a spare seat at the arena now. But they're still not satisfied. What with the Dominion championships being cancelled four years in a row, it's got us all wondering, will our gals ever be recognized as the best team in Canada? The Preston "Springs" Hotel is bettin' their money on it. We're cheering for you ladies, let's make the '38/'39 season one to remember.

(NELLIE approaches FACH.)

NELLIE. This is awkward.

FACH. If we don't have money, we can't tour. If we can't tour, we can't play.

NELLIE. We know.

FACH. So do our bank account a favor and just smile pretty for the cameras.

NELLIE. This is ridiculous.

FACH. What's the problem?

MARM. We're standing on the ice, not in the kitchen!

HELEN. Are we shooting a cover for the *Toronto Star* or the *Sears* catalogue?

MARM. "Satisfaction *not* guaranteed"!

HILDA. Can't we just play hockey?

FACH. It's just a few pictures for the paper, and a few for the Preston Springs card campaign.

WOMEN. What?!!

NELLIE. If I'm gonna be on someone's Christmas card, I wanna look like I know what I'm doing.

MARM. They're postcards.

NELLIE. I don't wanna know!

MARM. They're gonna sell them at the hotel.

NELLIE. I don't wanna know!!

MARM. I feel like I'm trying to sell someone a sweater.

HILDA. What about a shot of Marm throwing me into the boards?

MARM. Yeah!

HELEN. Or Hilda taking a mean slap shot?

FACH. It's taken me years to get this sponsorship money so don't –

MARM. I bet we're the only team in the world that didn't become national champions because they couldn't afford to play their final game.

NELLIE. Four times.

HILDA. I heard the Rustlers folded.

MARM. No!

HILDA. End of last season. And the London Silverwoods.

FACH. Would you stop with the chitchat and get / on with –

HELEN. What's the point of winning 250 games if we can't afford to play the one game that really counts.

(To the photographers.) You got your cameras ready, boys?

(To the **WOMEN**.*)* We do whatever it takes. No more defaults. No more cancelled championships. No folding. We're raising enough money to tour to Vancouver and back if we have to.

(To the photographers.) Hi, gentlemen. Thank you for coming. You know, before each game, us girls need to know we're hitting the ice prepared, so I like to make sure all my hockey equipment is securely fastened.

> *(She bends over to do her skate up, and the camera flashes.)*

NELLIE. Helen…

HELEN. Isn't that right girls?

(Another saucy pose for the camera as she pretends to do up her skate laces.)

MARM. *(Whispers to* **HILDA.***)* Whippet's not gonna like this postcard.

HILDA. He'll like it, he'll just want every copy.

HELEN. It can be a pretty dangerous game out there, fellas, and an ice skate to someone's jugular just isn't how we like to win.

> *(**NELLIE** tries to intercept her pose.)*

Now, watch goalie Nellie Ranscombe as she demonstrates one of the "tricks" of her trade. Give her a shot, Marm.

> *(**NELLIE** hits the splits with dramatic flair.)*

An incredible right pad save! She prefers the low ones boys.

HILDA. *(To* **MARM,** *under her breath.)* What does that mean?

MARM. I have no idea.

HELEN. Marmie, as we affectionately call her, isn't afraid to roll with the punches or throw a few. Show 'em a little rib cager.

> *(With a smile on her face,* **MARM** *gives* **HILDA** *a brutal elbow to the ribs.)*

HILDA. Awe!!

MARM. Oops.

HELEN. And who doesn't like a hip check or two once in a while?

> *(**MARM** lays a big hip check on* **HILDA.** *They hold it for the cameras.)*

HILDA. Hoh!

HELEN. As long as you're on the right end of it.

MARM. Any takers, gentlemen? ...I didn't think so.

HELEN. And there's nothing like watching Miss Hilda Ranscombe as she weaves her way through the defense. She's the fastest skater on the ice, that goes for men too boys. She'll stop on a dime and if a check takes her to the ice, she goes down with style and grace.

(**HILDA** *slides onto the ice and strikes a pose.*)

MARM. And let's not forget our fearless leader! For five whole seasons now! Our very own, Coach Pocket! Let the readers see who we get all our winning shots from.

FACH. I don't think so.

MARM. *(Tossing her stick to him.)* Have one, Fach.

FACH. *(Tosses it back.)* The article's not about me.

MARM. *(Holding out the stick.)* It's about the team, and you're a pretty special part of this team. Show us some "tricks" from your days out on the ice.

NELLIE. Give 'em your best shot!

HILDA.	**HELEN.**
Show us what you got, Coach.	Let's see it, Coach.

NELLIE. Come on, Coach!

MARM. I dare ya.

(**FACH** *takes the stick and tentatively sets up to take a shot. Finally, he takes an incredibly accurate wrist shot. He scores.*)

WOMEN. *(Amazed.)* Huh?! Whoa.

FACH. *(Hands the stick to* **MARM.***)* I'll stick to coaching.

(To the photographers.) That's probably enough wouldn't you say?

(To **HELEN.***)* Thank you...Helen.

(To the **WOMEN.***)* Now, go change!

(**HELEN** *and* **MARM** *leave.*)

NELLIE. Ask him.

HILDA. Now?

NELLIE. You promised.

HILDA. I know, but –

> (**NELLIE** *leaves.* **FACH** *cleans up after the shoot.*)

Coach? ...That was a really nice shot –

FACH. Go get changed, Ranscombe.

HILDA. You should get on the ice with us.

FACH. I don't think so.

HILDA. It'd be great practice for us, playing with someone who's got that hard a shot.

FACH. I don't have the right temperament for it.

HILDA. For practicing?

FACH. For playing. What do you want, Ranscombe?

HILDA. Oh, uh... I was...

FACH. What?

HILDA. It's alright.

FACH. Hilda.

HILDA. Nellie's been trying to – She thought you might have some ideas, being someone who works in – sports... I need a job.

FACH. Right.

HILDA. I'm not always good with... I've always helped out at home. They took me on at Preston Farms a couple summers, but you heard how that turned out... The men thought we were takin' their jobs.

FACH. Most girls – Women –

HILDA. I don't wanna be the one that doesn't contribute anymore. What I really want is – Maybe you could talk to someone. They could see me play. Try me out.

FACH. They?

HILDA. The NHL.

FACH. …It's a men's league.

HILDA. It's the only one that pays. I don't wanna leave the Rivulettes – but if that's the only option. Do you think I could make it?

FACH. …What about teaching the kids? Make a bit of money doing that.

HILDA. Classrooms make me nervous, Mr. Fach, I don't –

FACH. To skate. You don't need a classroom. You teach them on the ice.

HILDA. Oh… Sure… I can do that, I can teach them to skate.

FACH. I just have to get a few kids signed up.

HILDA. Oh.

FACH. But when I do I'll – I'll let you know.

HILDA. Thanks Coach. And please don't say anything about the – You're right, it's a men's league, why would they ever…

FACH. If they did, it'd be you.

HILDA. Thanks.

(**HILDA** *leaves…*)

Scene Fourteen
Taking Sides

(**HELEN**, **MARM**, *and* **NELLIE** *at the Wragge Shoe Company.*)

RADIO ANNOUNCER. And a disturbing turn of events, the MS St. Louis that set out from Hamburg has been denied permission to enter the United States. Captain Schroder and the 900 Jewish refugees on board are now forced to turn back and are looking to Belgium, the UK and other European countries to provide sanctuary. We'll keep you informed on that story as it progresses. Stay tuned for local news up next, here on your CBC.

(**MARM** *turns off the radio.*)

MARM. There's plenty of room here.

HELEN. You heard our Prime Minister, "None is too many."

MARM. What side do you think Fach is on?

NELLIE. Marm.

MARM. The German side obviously.

NELLIE. You can't assume that.

MARM. He probably doesn't even like Jews, that's why he was in that camp, / they found out –

HELEN. Oh my gosh.

NELLIE. They're not going to put a German in a Canadian camp because he doesn't like Jews, they're going to put him there because they think he's a threat to Canadians.

MARM. We *are* Canadians.

NELLIE. All Canadians not just, Jewish ones.

HELEN. He's our coach.

MARM. It was supposed to be getting better, not worse. I should have gone to Montreal and volunteered for Annie when I had the chance, instead of staying here and –

HELEN. You could've gone. I didn't tell you to –

MARM. And abandon our parents while you're off marrying some Catholic Army boy.

HELEN. That was four years ago!

MARM. I'll have to marry the most Jewish man ever to make up for what you did.

NELLIE. Sigmund Freud?

MARM. More Jewish.

NELLIE. Albert Einstein?

MARM. More Jewish.

NELLIE. Jesus.

MARM. More alive.

NELLIE. I could have gone to school, finished my degree, and then made back the money I'd lost going to school in the first place.

HELEN. So go now.

MARM. Way to rub it in, Helen.

HELEN. People are making it work.

NELLIE. Where? You got married, and you're still working.

HELEN. What else would I do all day?

NELLIE. Is that what you tell Whippet? Because I know you wouldn't be working if you didn't have to. If Hilda would get a job –

MARM. Why doesn't she?

NELLIE. ...It's not easy for her.

MARM. She's not dumb.

NELLIE. It's not about that. She gets things mixed up – In the wrong order or – Numbers mostly. It's like she sees it differently than us, who knows – She's terrified of getting a job and then not being able to do it.

HELEN. Maybe she'll marry George –

(**NELLIE** *and* **MARM** *laugh.*)

...And then you'll be free to do whatever you choose.

MARM. Fat chance.

HELEN. I don't know about that.

MARM. The only thing Hilda wants to marry is her hockey stick.

HELEN. Jealous?

MARM. Of George Williams? Not Jewish enough.

NELLIE. Yesterday on the radio when they were talking to Bobbie Rosenfeld about women's hockey going to the Olympics.

MARM. What?

NELLIE. All hypothetical. Hilda was so excited she had to go skate laps along the river to calm herself down.

MARM. Imagine if she's right?

NELLIE. What women are playing hockey besides us and the Americans?

HELEN. Maybe it wasn't the Olympics at all, *maybe* she was excited about something else.

(**HILDA** *enters, holding a newspaper.*)

HILDA. *(Only expecting* **HELEN.***)* Hi.

HELEN. Finally! I couldn't keep my mouth shut any longer.

HILDA. I didn't realize you were all working today.

HELEN. What happened? …When Whippet asked me I was so nervous I said yes before he even popped the question. My face turned bright red.

NELLIE. George?! You told Helen and not me?

HELEN. She borrowed a dress.

NELLIE. Well?

HILDA. …

MARM. Hockey stick.

HELEN. You said no?

HILDA. I had to.

HELEN. But he's got a job now. He makes a 1,000 a year.

HILDA. It's in the paper today.

NELLIE. Hilda.

HILDA. *(To* **NELLIE.***)* Not just on the radio. It's right here! Look!

(Giving **NELLIE** *the paper.)* PJ Mulqueen, the head of the Canadian Olympic committee said they want the best in Canada. It could be us. If we win the Dominion title it will be us.

HELEN. You turned down a marriage proposal for a hockey game?

HILDA. It's not just a hockey game.

HELEN. You can have both.

NELLIE. We're not all meant to be someone's wife.

HELEN. Of course not but –

HILDA. Don't you see how big this is? We could get our own professional league! Be paid!

HILDA. *(Leaving.)* I'm gonna hit the ice. We got two games in Montreal this weekend. They're fighting for the title too.

(Stopping herself.) Please don't be disappointed in me... Maybe I'm fooling myself and maybe this *is* all hypothetical, but there's still a chance that it's not.

(**HILDA** *exits.*)

MARM. ...She is right... There is a chance.

NELLIE. Until someone officially asks us, it's just talk... I'm gonna give her someone to shoot at.

MARM. It's not five o'clock.

NELLIE. Close enough.

(**NELLIE** *leaves.*)

MARM. ...A bunch of hockey dolls going to the Olympics? Could that really happen?

HELEN. I guess we'll find out.

MARM. Gotta win that title!

HELEN. Marm!...

> (**MARM** *leaves.* **HELEN** *turns on the radio to distract herself until work is over. Music plays,* * *then...*)

RADIO. That was *[title of chosen song]*. And in breaking news from overseas, in response to Nazi Germany's defiance of the Munich Agreement and occupation of Czechoslovakia, the United Kingdom has assured the support of itself and France to guarantee Polish

---

*A license to produce *Glory* does not include a performance license for any third-party or copyrighted music. Licensees should create an original composition or use music in the public domain. For further information, please see Music and Third-Party Materials Use Note on page iii.

defense in the case of German aggression. His Majesty's Government feel themselves bound at once to lend the Polish government the support of the entire British Empire.

Scene Fifteen
Taking on Montreal

ANIMATEUR. Mesdames et messieurs, bienvenue au Forum de Montréal qui héberge VOTRE équipe de hockey préférée. Une équipe qui connaît d'ailleurs une saison sans tache, n'ayant perdu aucun match jusqu'à maintenant, vous les aimez, les exceptionnels Maroons de Montréal ! Aujourd'hui, Montréal accueille, les champions de l'Est des cinq dernières saisons, une équipe vite sur leurs patins, le tir solide, les grandes Dames de la patinoire, les Preston Springs Rivulettes!

[Ladies and Gentleman! Welcome to the Montreal Forum! The home of your local hockey sweethearts, leading the season with a spotless record, having not lost a single game all season, the exceptional Montreal Maroons! And today we welcome to our fair city, a much celebrated team from our neighboring province, the Eastern champs for the last five seasons, the fast skating, sharpshooting, ladies of the rink, the Preston Springs Rivulettes!]

> (**FACH** *heads to the boards.* **HILDA** *and* **NELLIE** *are in a deep discussion by the net.*)

FACH. Three hundred fans in the forum? We filled this place last year.

> (**HILDA** *skates over to* **FACH**.)

HILDA. Helen's not playing!

FACH. I just saw her.

NELLIE. She didn't get off the train.

HILDA. Maybe, Whippet thought two hockey games in a row was too much.

FACH. Too much for what?

HILDA. For Helen.

FACH. Great.

NELLIE. What are we supposed to do?

FACH. ...Gladys'll start.

HILDA. Gladys is fourteen.

FACH. Don't tell me Marm went with her?

NELLIE. Locker room.

FACH. We gotta! – Gather in! Irene Wall is in net. She hasn't been scored on all season. To say she's confident, is an understatement. So we gotta be creative out there. Give her every shot you got.

> (**HILDA** *and* **NELLIE** *skate onto the ice.*)

HILDA. I thought Helen could have both.

> (**MARM** *enters and goes right to her position.*)

MARM. Coach.

FACH. You're late!

> (*The Rivulettes vs. The Montreal Maroons.*)

> (*Music: Game Five.* The team is overcompensating for* **HELEN***'s absence, and* **NELLIE** *is distracted.* **MARM** *becomes quite aggressive.*)

ANIMATEUR. Quatre minutes depuis le début de la période et Preston est pris dans sa zone. [We're four minutes in and Preston is bottled up in their own end.]

FACH. Spread out!

---

*A license to produce *Glory* does not include a performance license for any third-party or copyrighted music. Licensees should create an original composition or use music in the public domain. For further information, please see Music and Third-Party Materials Use Note on page iii.

ANIMATEUR. Simone Couchon arrive avec la rondelle pour les Maroons. Elle s'élance vers le filet La rondelle est récupérée par Nellie Ranscombe! [Simone Couchon comes up with the puck for the Maroons. She takes a shot. Great save by Nellie Ranscombe!]

MARM. *(Cross-checking Wright into the boards.)* Did you do it?!

HILDA. Marm!

ANIMATEUR. Ooo, Marm Schmuck rentre dans la bande. [Ooo, Schmuck drills her into the boards.]

*(Whistle: Penalty to **MARM**.)*

Elle se rend u banc des pénalités. [She'll go to the penalty box for that.]

FACH. What was that about?

MARM. She was in the way.

FACH. You charged her from the other side of the ice!

(Whistle: Game on.)

Now you got Hilda killing a penalty for you.

ANIMATEUR. Simone Couchon se dirige vers le filet avec la rondelle. Ranscombe essaye de lui enlever. Couchon passe derrière le filet. Revient devant, en jouant la défensive. [Couchon again with the puck, Ranscombe trying to take it from her. Couchon, from behind the net...with the rubber under her stick.]

FACH. Get in front of it!

ANIMATEUR. Lance, et compte! Magnifique tir dans le coin supérieur. Un à zéro pour les Maroons! [Shoots! *SCORES!* Flicking the puck into the top corner. It's one-zero Maroons.]

(Whistle: Maroons score.)

(**NELLIE** *hits the ice with her stick.* **MARM** *skates back onto the ice.*)

FACH. *(To* **MARM.***)* Was it worth it?!

(To the team.) Alright, come on. Let's get one back.

(Whistle: Game on.)

ANIMATEUR. Quinze minutes écoulés dans cette deuxième période. Attaque de l'équipe Preston. Mais la gardienne Irene Wall reste invincible. Leclair va revenir en sens inverse. [Fifteen minutes into the second period. Preston on the attack, but Irene Wall is invincible. Leclair back the other way now.]

FACH. Get back! Get back! Who's on her?!

MARM. *(Hits Leclair into the boards.)* Was it you?

FACH. Careful Schmuck!

ANIMATEUR. Solide mise en échec de Schmuck sur Leclair. LeGiroux a la voie libre pour les Maroons. C'est l'échappée. Elle tire. Et marque! Deux à zéro Montréal. [Schmuck hitting Leclair hard into the boards! Leaving Giroux wide open for the Maroons. She shoots! She scores! Two–zero Montreal!]

(Whistle: Montreal scores.)

(**NELLIE** *hits the ice with her stick again.*)

(Intermission: They skate over to the boards.)

FACH. We're not gonna make it to the final if you keep playing like that!

HILDA. Our rhythm's all off.

NELLIE. Doesn't feel right with Helen not here.

FACH. It's not personal.

NELLIE. Course it's personal.

FACH. It's not gonna help you win the game.

(*To* **MARM**.) Are you gonna tell me what's going on?

MARM. I'm playing hard out there!

FACH. Too hard! You're gonna hurt someone. Keep your temperament in check.

(*To the team.*) A little less drama, ladies, and a little more game. The Wall's still standing and we're down two-zip.

(*Whistle: Game back on.*)

ANIMATEUR. Autour de Hilda Ranscombe de remonter. Elles entrent en zone des Maroons. Des joulets défensives – [Here comes Hilda Ranscombe, a solo effort, stick-handling through the defense, in on –]

MARM. Hilda! I'm open! / Pass! Hilda! Over here!

ANIMATEUR. Elles se retrouvent derrière la gardienne Irene Wall. Tirs quand même mais la rondelle effleure le côté du filet. Maroons deux, Preston zéro, à la fin de la deuxième période. [She tries to tuck it behind Irene Wall. She tries a shot but hits the side of the net! Maroons two, Preston one, at the end of the second period.]

(*Whistle: Save by Wall.*)

MARM. I was right there.

HILDA. I had it!

MARM. I was wide open!

NELLIE. Play together out there!

(*Whistle: Game back on.*)

ANIMATEUR. Troisième période, la tension monte. [Third Period, the tension is mounting.]

MARM. Hilda! Hilda, here!

(**MARM** *elbows Betsy Goddard in the face.*)

Agh! Take it down!

ANIMATEUR. Aouu, Schmuck frappe Betsy Goodard au visage avec le coude. [Oof! Right on the nose! Betsy Goddard taking the elbow of Marm Schmuck.]

(*Whistle: Penalty to* **MARM**.)

FACH. What are you doing Schmuck?!

ANIMATEUR. Le jeu se durcit. Les Maroons semblent s'essouffler face aux Rivulettes. [That's a major for some rough play. The Rivulettes wearing down the Maroons.]

FACH. You're falling apart ladies! Get your heads in the game, your eyes on the puck, and *you*, leave the hittin' to someone else!

(*Whistle: Game back on.*)

(**MARM** *in the penalty box.*)

What was that?!

MARM. …

FACH. You not talkin' to me?…

(**MARM** *springs out of the box.*)

ANIMATEUR. Changement. Schmuck revient sur la glace face à Gladys Hawkins qui renvoit Schmuck. Elle lance, et compte! [Schmuck out of the box, to Gladys Hawkins back to Schmuck. She shoots. *SCORES!*]

(*Whistle:* **MARM** *scores.*)

MARM. Yahhhhh!!

FACH. That's more like it!

ANIMATEUR. Deux-un Maroons! [Two–one Maroons!]

(Whistle: Game on.)

ANIMATEUR. Ranscombe qui passe à Hawkins qui passe à Schmuck. Elle prend la vitesse soufe au fil, et marque! Deux buts en moins d'une minute pour Schmuck. Le match est à égalité. [Ranscombe to Hawkins to Schmuck. She winds up, SCORES! That's two goals in under a minute for Schmuck!! The game is tied at two!!]

MARM. Hahaaa!!

(Whistle: **MARM** *scores.)*

FACH. There ya go!

ANIMATEUR. Deux buts en moins d'une minute pour Schmuck. Le match est à égalité. [That's two goals in under a minute for Schmuck!! The game is tied at two!!]

FACH. Schmuckie's got us back in this one! Don't let her down.

(Whistle: Game on.)

ANIMATEUR. Les Maroons ont des avantages numériques. Ranscombe s'en part de la rondelle. Elle déjoue l'offensive des Maroons à la manière d'Aurèle Joliat. Décoche un tir puissant, et c'est le but! [Maroons short-handed. Ranscombe, looking like Aurele Jolia out there, stick-handling through the entire Maroon line and that is – IN THE NET!!]

(Whistle: **HILDA** *scores, game over.)*

Et c'est la fin du match. Quelle performance de Hilda Ranscombe. [The game is over! What a performance by Hilda Ranscombe!]

(In English, with French accent.) Hey, Mademoiselle Ranscombe! I'm calling the NHL! Who cares if you're a woman! I would sign you!

MARM. I score twice and you're off to the NHL?

HILDA. *(Laughing.)* He wasn't serious.

MARM. *(Pushing* **HILDA.***)* It's not funny!

NELLIE. Marm!

HILDA. What's wrong with you?

MARM. *(Going after* **HILDA.***)* Why you always gotta be better than the rest of us?

NELLIE. *(Holding* **MARM** *back.)* We won the game.

MARM. *She* won the game!

FACH. *(Grabbing* **MARM** *by the arm.)* What's going on?

MARM. Let go of me.

FACH. Stop it! Now!

MARM. I'm just as good as Hilda!

FACH. You gonna prove that by fighting? You gonna push her into the boards? Break her wrist so she can't shoot?

MARM. No.

FACH. I know what it's like to take your personal frustration out on the ice.

MARM. That's not what I was doing.

FACH. I *know* what it can do.

MARM. …

FACH. Those hits were dirty.

MARM. Does it matter?

FACH. Is this about Helen?

MARM. Can't it be about me?! And anyone else like me, that reads the sign out front that says, "No Dogs or Jews allowed"! It's not enough that they won't let me in to university, I can't leave the job I hate, I'm told I can't play hockey either?

FACH. ...I'm sorry.

MARM. Not enough to tear it down! Not enough to tell the league it's unacceptable!

FACH. I didn't see it.

MARM. What about you? Did you see it?

HILDA.	NELLIE.
No.	I didn't.

MARM. You're my coach! You're supposed to look out for me! I don't care if you *are* German!

FACH. ...What do you want me to say?

MARM. I don't want you to *say* anything. I want you to *do* something, 'cause apparently, I'm not allowed.

(**MARM** *storms out.*)

NELLIE. Marm.

(**NELLIE** *goes after her, leaving* **HILDA** *and* **FACH** *in awkward silence.*)

Scene Sixteen
In the Papers

(**NELLIE** *and* **HELEN** *at the Wragge Shoe Company.*)

RADIO ANNOUNCER. And in women's hockey, the Preston Rivulettes defeated the Maroon girls of Montreal, three to two, this weekend, at the Forum. Playing without power forward Helen Schmuck, the Rivulettes pulled off a narrow escape from a game that looked to be sown up by their rivals. Preston moves on to the Eastern Canada finals where they'll play the Toronto Ladies, for a place in the Dominion Championships. A date will be set once one of the two teams is able to secure ice time.

If you're just joining us, this is CBC Radio, Canada's source of free entertainment and news from across the country and abroad. As conflict looms, CBC correspondent / Graham Spry looks at Britain's readiness for war and what that means for our Canadian troops.

HELEN. Turn it off! I'm sick of hearing about it already. I'd rather listen to the Ontario Farm Report twenty-four hours a day. It's not even free entertainment. We're taxed $2.50, whether we listen to it or not.

NELLIE. How would they even know who was listening? They peakin' in people's windows at night?

HELEN. ...Marm told me what happened.

NELLIE. Ya... I didn't see it.

HELEN. Gladys Hawkins, huh?

NELLIE. She did alright.

HELEN. *(Picks up the paper.)* "Even with the substitution of young Hawkins, the Rivulettes remain the best stick-handlers in the women's hockey realm." ...She's good.

NELLIE. She's learning.

HELEN. "Nellie Ranscombe in goal is a supreme / performer."

NELLIE. You can skip that part.

HELEN. "Coach Fach iced a well-drilled team outsmarting a wall of a goalie having a record-breaking season."

NELLIE. Jealous?

HELEN. Sounds like you're taking care of business without me.

NELLIE. We're so close. Would you just play.

HELEN. I don't want to jeopardize the well-drilled team.

NELLIE. You are the team!

HELEN. We're trying to have a baby.

NELLIE. ...Oh.

HELEN. Oh? That's it?

NELLIE. Sorry. It's great.

HELEN. What's going on?

NELLIE. He's too controlling. He met you when you were a player, he shouldn't expect you to stop / because –

HELEN. He doesn't. It was my decision. I decided to stop playing.

NELLIE. Why?

HELEN. There might be a war, Nell.

NELLIE. Not here.

HELEN. Whippet's Army.

NELLIE. Canadian Army.

HELEN. Doesn't matter.

NELLIE. What's going on over there has nothing to do with us!

HELEN. Maybe I don't love it the same way you do.

NELLIE. You think I love being shot at, game after game?

HELEN. You're the best in the league.

NELLIE. And I'm still scared of the puck! You wanna – My brothers used to take shots at me when I was a kid. They tied cushions to me. Stuck me in net. I didn't know it was a game. I'd run home crying, with a face full of blood.

HELEN. I'm sorry, Nell.

NELLIE. The game is – It's not the same without you. It's the team, I love. You.

HELEN. ...You deserve to have the paper say nice things about you.

NELLIE. ...And you don't deserve what they said about you.

HELEN. What did they say? Where?!

(Reading from the paper.) "Helen Schmuck's unsparing efforts lowered her vitality and resistance so much that she suffered a breakdown." That's ridiculous! "A fragile woman who wasn't made to play such an aggressive sport." After this many years?! Have we proved nothing?!

NELLIE. The battle's not over.

HELEN. Will it ever be?

NELLIE. Not without you.

HELEN. ...Hey... You showed me that on purpose.

Scene Seventeen
Anything Besides Hockey

(**HILDA** *rushes into the arena to find* **FACH** *repairing a hockey net.*)

HILDA. Coach!

FACH. *(Startled.)* Geezuz, Hilda!

HILDA. Sorry. Did you talk to Mr. Mulqueen?

FACH. I'm surprised you weren't listening in on the conversation.

HILDA. What did they say?

FACH. ...The committee wants to make it happen.

HILDA. Really?!

FACH. Canada, the US, they're both agreed.

HILDA. The Olympics?! Really?!

FACH. But they need to raise the level of play outside of America.

HILDA. In the paper today it said the Rivulettes are the top contender to go.

FACH. They want an exhibition tour. The European Hockey Association.

HILDA. What?

FACH. France, Switzerland, Norway. To show the women of Europe where we're at. With the Rivulettes' record and experience, they're hoping it's you.

HILDA. Hoping?

FACH. They want the Dominion Champions. If that's you, then –

HILDA. It can't be the Rustlers.

FACH. No, but Calgary and Winnipeg are both strong in the West. Toronto, if you don't beat them tomorrow.

HILDA. We've never lost to Toronto. Their offense is slow, their D is patchy, they always think they're better than they really are.

FACH. I just don't want you getting ahead of yourself. If we don't win the Dominion title, we're not going anywhere. Without Helen the team's not as strong up front. Marm's... Nellie's distracted.

HILDA. I'll get us there.

FACH. The whole team needs to get you there.

HILDA. Helen wants this just as much as I do. She'd never miss a chance like this.

FACH. People change, Hilda.

HILDA. I'll talk to her! I'll –

FACH. Hilda! You gotta – ! Don't you have any... Things that – Anything besides hockey?

HILDA. I don't understand.

FACH. You're doing a great job teaching those kids. I know it's not exactly what you want but you've got a real knack for –

HILDA. I need to be a part of this, Coach. The future of – this sport. Yes, I want to win the Dominion title, I want that more than anything, but then what? What happens next? If the Olympics are gonna happen, I have to be there. I have to be a part of that.

FACH. Then get your team together captain. You got two big games to win.

> (**HILDA** *leaves.*)

Scene Eighteen
What Team Are You On?

ANNOUNCER. Hello out there and welcome back to the Galt Arena and the finals of the Eastern Ladies' Hockey Championships! Where your home team, the Preston Rivulettes are taking on the big city, Toronto Ladies.

> *(MARM is warming up, and NELLIE is tightening her pads on the bench.)*

MARM. Norway? Switzerland?! Finland!! Not Germany obviously. Sweden!

NELLIE. I can't get excited until we know for sure.

MARM. It has to be us! It has to. Can you imagine?!

NELLIE. Let's just beat Toronto first.

MARM. I gotta get outta here. This town is getting smaller and smaller. I get menstrual cramps, and everyone knows.

NELLIE. Come on.

MARM. I go for a walk at night, and I'm judged for walking too quickly.

NELLIE. I go for a walk and no one notices. Which would you prefer?

MARM. You know, we could be Toronto Ladies. Say money is no object.

NELLIE. We can dream.

MARM. I'm serious! You're a smart woman, Nell. You can go wherever you want. Let's do it. You can go to university. I'll pound on the door until they finally let me in.

NELLIE. I'm not playing for the Toronto Ladies.

MARM. Course not but we could invade their city. We beat Toronto. We win the Dominion Championships, we go to Europe! And then we get outta here.

NELLIE. What about Helen?

MARM. She's not going anywhere.

NELLIE. She's your sister.

MARM. Would you rather go with her?

NELLIE. Wouldn't it be strange for you? To be so far away?

MARM. No. Would it be strange for you?

NELLIE. I don't know.

MARM. Do you love her?

NELLIE. Marm!

MARM. It's not / bad.

NELLIE. Stop it!

MARM. I don't think it's weird.

NELLIE. I saw it. The sign in Montreal... I didn't know what to do so I pretended I didn't.

MARM. ...It's fine.

NELLIE. No it's not. I should've torn it down, I should've –

(**HILDA** *enters.*)

HILDA. Ready for this?

MARM. You bet.

NELLIE. Yup!

HILDA. We on the same team tonight, Marmie?

MARM. Of course.

HILDA. Helen's not here... I tried, but – I've been working with Gladys. Her passing's getting better. She's a good stick-handler. If we handle the scoring, Marmie, I know we can win this.

MARM. ...Then let's go score some goals!

(**MARM** *heads to the ice,* **NELLIE** *and* **HILDA** *check in with each other about* **MARM** *and then skate into position.*)

(*The Rivulettes vs. The Toronto Ladies.*)

(*Whistle: Game on.*)

(**FACH** *enters.*)

FACH. Lets go ladies!

(*Music: Game Six.* * *Concentrated. There is still an inner competitiveness, but they share the ultimate goal of winning.*)

ANNOUNCER. Deep in the first period. We're tied at one. The Toronto Ladies looking to give the Rivulettes their first loss in five years! Marm Schmuck with the puck, Ranscombe on the wing.

HILDA. Marmie!

FACH. You got Hilda, Schmuckie. Use her!

ANNOUNCER. Schmuck shoots, she *SCORES!*

(*Whistle:* **MARM** *scores.*)

FACH. Beautiful!

ANNOUNCER. Marm Schmuck with a fantastic wrist shot.

FACH. (*Clapping.*) Nice work, Schmuckie!

(*Whistle: Game on.*)

ANNOUNCER. Now it's Hilda Ranscombe with the puck, the team favorite racing up ice, she winds up, *SCORES!*

---

*A license to produce *Glory* does not include a performance license for any third-party or copyrighted music. Licensees should create an original composition or use music in the public domain. For further information, please see Music and Third-Party Materials Use Note on page iii.

(Whistle: **HILDA** *scores.)*

FACH. *(Clapping but with a little less enthusiasm.)* Way to go, Ranscombe. Way to go.

(Whistle: Game picks up.)

ANNOUNCER. Dora Grant for Toronto now, moving in on the Rivulettes' goal. Nellie Ranscombe has been solid in goal.

FACH.	**NELLIE.**
Who's on her?	Come on! Come on!

NELLIE. Get back!

ANNOUNCER. Grant shoots! *SCORES!*

(Whistle: Toronto Ladies score.)

Ranscombe not able to get her pads down. Looking a little rattled. Toronto trailing by one now.

FACH. You alright in there, Ranscombe?

NELLIE. ...Fine.

(Whistle: Game back on.)

ANNOUNCER. Schmuck and Ranscombe moving in... Schmuck shoots! Rebound to Ranscombe, shoots! Off the post. Schmuck after it, Ranscombe's calling for it –

FACH. You're on the same team, remember?!

ANNOUNCER. – Schmuck in alone. Schmuck shoots. Schmuck with the rebound! Schmuck with the shot. Schmuck *SCORES!*

(Whistle: **MARM** *scores.)*

Schmuckity, Schmuck, Schmuck! Listen to me eh?! Soundin' all Jewish up here!

*(***MARM*** *stops and looks up at the* **ANNOUNCER.**)*

MARM. *(To the* ANNOUNCER.*)* And what does that sound like?

FACH. Marm.

MARM. That sound funny to you?!

HILDA. Marm!

(HILDA *and* NELLIE *hold* MARM *back.*)

MARM. What else ya think is funny? You think me playing hockey is funny? Did I miss the sign out front?

FACH. That's not what's / going on here!

MARM. Gonna start another riot at Christie Pits?!

FACH. Alright.

(FACH *walks onto the ice.*)

MARM. Do something, Fach!

FACH. Get off the ice!

MARM. That's right, just kick the Jew off the ice, make your country proud.

(MARM *storms off,* FACH *follows her.*)

HILDA. It's the Eastern Finals! ...Norma! You're on for Marm. Let's go ladies!

Scene Nineteen
The Pits

(**MARM** *enters the locker room,* **FACH** *follows.*)

MARM. Get out.

FACH. You think you're the only one who's ever been judged?

MARM. Get outta here!

FACH. Insulted?

MARM. Why do you hate me so much?

FACH. What kind of question is that?

MARM. I've read about people like you, who have these secret lives. Pretending to be one thing in public –

FACH. Pretending what?!

MARM. But really you're a part of these underground – I know what they're doing in your country.

FACH. This is my country! I was born here! Just like you!

MARM. Then why'd they arrest you?

FACH. What?

MARM. Lock you up in that camp?

FACH. …

MARM. You think we didn't know?

(**FACH** *takes a moment, not sure where to start*)

FACH. During the war…my parents were suspected of being enemy aliens. So they were interned. After being invited – recruited to immigrate here. They'd been here for thirty years. They didn't know what was going on. They hardly spoke English. So, I defended them. And I became a suspect too. I wasn't much older than you when I was… Do you have any idea what it was like at that camp?

MARM. No.

FACH. No one ever should. Our country does horrible things too. As you know. Now, can we go play hockey?

MARM. So I can be laughed at? Made to feel like I'm not good enough?

FACH. You're playing in the Eastern Finals, Miss Schmuck! Not him! Not me! You! Don't let your anger for whatever bullshit is happening in the world ruin what's really important. You've earned the right to play. This team needs you to play.

> (**FACH** *holds out* **MARM***'s stick for her.*)

MARM. Just once, I'd like to know how it feels to be number one.

FACH. Me too! Now, can we skip out on confession and go win a hockey game?

MARM. *(Taking the stick.)* Jews don't have confession.

FACH. *(Follows her.)* Maybe I'll convert.

> *(Rivulettes vs. Toronto Ladies continued.)*
>
> *(Whistle: Game on.)*
>
> *(The action of the final seconds of the game plays out.)*

ANNOUNCER. It's Hilda Ranscombe up ice now. We're into the final seconds. She's pushed into the corner by Toronto. Trying to hold onto the puck. Fifteen seconds now.

MARM. Norma!

ANNOUNCER. Marm Schmuck back on the ice.

HILDA. Marm!

FACH. Move the puck around!

MARM. Here!

ANNOUNCER. Ranscombe managing to get the puck to Schmuck. Who crosses behind the net. Five seconds.

NELLIE. Take it home girls!

FACH. In front!

ANNOUNCER. Ranscombe in front now. Schmuck to Ranscombe back to Schmuck.

FACH. Shoot!

ANNOUNCER. She scores!!!!

(Whistle: Scores, game over.)

FACH. Yessss!!!! Yehheesssss!!!

*(**HILDA** swoops in on **MARM** and picks her up. **NELLIE** joins them.)*

ANNOUNCER. Marm Schmuck with the beautiful pass from Hilda Ranscombe and the Preston Rivulettes have won the hockey game. Once again they are your Eastern champions! The Dominion title is within reach. And in September they will finally get their chance! For the first time in four years! They will battle for the honor of becoming Canada's best!

Scene Twenty
Part of Our Game

(**NELLIE** *and* **MARM** *in the locker room.*)

MARM. I just need to know the name and then I'll be fine. I wanna know who they are, I wanna know how they play, and then I wanna create an air-tight, goal-proof, winning strategy, so we can destroy them.

NELLIE. Something feels weird.

MARM. What?

NELLIE. ...Is this the first time we've ever practiced during the day?

MARM. ...By day do you mean, at a time when there's daylight?

NELLIE. Uh-huh.

MARM. ...Yup.

NELLIE. The men's team must have cancelled.

(**HILDA** *rushes in.*)

MARM. Who is it?

HILDA. The Winnipeg Eatons!

MARM & NELLIE. Eatons?

HILDA. The girls all work for the department store.

MARM.	NELLIE.
You're kidding.	Really?

MARM. Do they get a lot of penalties for *charging*?

HILDA. Eleven.

NELLIE. In one game?!

HILDA. They're tough. Quick stick-handlers, fast skaters. Yvette Lambert, plays for them.

MARM. Scarface?!

NELLIE. I read about that!

MARM. Her nose was like a flap.

NELLIE. Hanging on by this one piece of skin.

MARM. Helen would quit if she hadn't already.

HILDA. They had three thousand fans at their last game.

NELLIE. They're good.

HILDA. Lambert's scored sixty-one goals this season. And Manson stopped that many shots in one game.

NELLIE. They're really good.

HILDA. They didn't lose a game all season.

NELLIE. They're unbeatable.

MARM. My Olympic dream just crumbled a bit.

HILDA. We're unbeatable too. We just gotta play our game. If we think about what's at stake, at –

> **(HELEN** *bursts in.)*

HELEN. I wanna play!

MARM.	**HILDA.**
Hey.	What?

NELLIE. Helen.

HELEN. …I just thought that… I didn't… I'm not fragile! I've been nailing girls into the boards for seven years! And there's still idiots at national newspapers saying this sport is too aggressive for us?! Our bodies are too delicate? There's nothing delicate or fragile about any of us. My muscles do bulge a bit now and I've got used to it. I even like them… What we fight for on that ice, is so much bigger than the game. The criticism, the jokes, the put-downs, the men who think we can't compete, the women who think we shouldn't. It's all part of it right? Playing while you're trying to have a baby, is part of our game. It's not the same as the men's, because when we fight to win, there's a whole lot more at stake.

NELLIE. ...So put your skates on. We gotta practice up.

HILDA. We're playing the Winnipeg Eatons.

MARM. They can skate and shop.

HELEN. It's not too late?

(**FACH** *comes in.*)

FACH. Ladies! There's a fresh sheet of ice out there!

(*Seeing* **HELEN.**) Have you came to your senses?

HELEN. Yes.

FACH. Good... Are we practicing or what? Those Eatons wanna open a store overseas and I wanna put them out of business.

MARM. You think I'm gonna let Scarface go to Europe before me?

HELEN. Who's Scarface?

HILDA & MARM. No one!

Scene Twenty-One
Game Changing

(Maple Leaf Gardens. The **WOMEN** *warm up. For a moment,* **HILDA** *looks toward the net at the end of the rink and makes a silent vow not to miss this time.)*

FOSTER HEWITT. Hello Canada and Hockey fans in the United States and Newfoundland. Welcome to Maple Leaf Gardens, the home of your 1939 Dominion Championships!! For several years now women have taken to hockey, a rather strenuous game for the fair sex, but it is astonishing how dexterous these lipstick "puck tossers" have become. Today we welcome the visiting team, the Western champions, the Winnipeg Eatons!

(The **WOMEN** *stop and look toward the Eatons' end.)*

And playing in front of a crowd of five thousand fans. The six-time winners of the Eastern Championships, your Preston Rivulettes!

(The **WOMEN** *skate to the blue line and look out to their fans. They break to skate over to the bench,* **HELEN** *looks for Whippet in the crowd.)*

HELEN. Hilda, something's wrong. Whippet's not in his seat.

HILDA. Don't worry. He's probably getting a drink.

*(***FACH** *enters, distracted.)*

FACH. Alright listen up! The Germans have come a long way for this game, so they're gonna come out strong.

HILDA. We're playing the Eatons.

FACH. What I say?

NELLIE. The Germans.

FACH. *(Laughs it off.)* I want the win so bad, I'm not thinking straight. It's taken us five seasons but here we are. You've got an entire country cheering for you, or at least half of one. If there was a time to leave it all on the ice, it's now. Play your game out there. The game that got you here. Fast skating. Crisp shooting. Solid goaltending. Let's show those department store recruits what we're sellin'!

HILDA. Ri-Vu–

ALL. Let's go!

> *(The Rivulettes vs. The Winnipeg Eatons.)*
>
> *(Music: Game Seven.* The* **TEAM** *plays with dynamic determination.)*

FOSTER HEWITT. Schmuck wins the face-off.

HILDA. Marm!

FOSTER HEWITT. To Ranscombe. She turns, and sails down the ice.

HELEN. Hilda!

FOSTER HEWITT. Cross-ice pass to Schmuck!

NELLIE. SHOOT!!!!

FOSTER HEWITT. Nice save by Paskiman! The Eatons back the other way now!

FACH. Get back ladies!

FOSTER HEWITT. Nellie Ranscombe dives towards the puck! Did you see that?! / What a stop by the Preston goalie.

---

*A license to produce *Glory* does not include a performance license for any third-party or copyrighted music. Licensees should create an original composition or use music in the public domain. For further information, please see Music and Third-Party Materials Use Note on page iii.

FACH. Beautiful stop Nellie!

FOSTER HEWITT. These girls have brought a little fuel from their last Dominion title fire. A disheartening loss – Helen Schmuck shoots!

FACH. That a girl!

FOSTER HEWITT. Hits the post!

FACH. Keep the pressure on!

FOSTER HEWITT. Winnipeg now charging up the ice.

FACH. Get on her!

FOSTER HEWITT. Ranscombe holds her ground. Both teams banging away at the puck!

FACH. Get it outta there!

FOSTER HEWITT. Preston wrestling the puck away.

HELEN. *(Getting hit.)* Ugh!!

FACH. What was that?

HILDA. *(Getting thrown to the ice.)* Agh

> *(Whistle: Fight.)*

> **(HILDA** *is dumped onto the ice.* **NELLIE** *pulls the Eatons player off of her.* **HELEN** *fights a player against the boards.* **MARM** *circles, wrestles a player, gets some punches in.)*

FOSTER HEWITT. Sticks are flying! Tempers are flaring! Eva Smith, for the Eatons, dumps Hilda Ranscombe to the ice. Now proceeds to pummel the local player. Referee Wright steps in to disengage the players and dole out penalties.

FACH. Alright, ladies! Take it out on the scoreboard not on each other!!

> *(Whistle: First intermission.)*

HILDA. I can't get any shots through.

FACH. They're strong defensively. You gotta find a way around them. You can't lose your heads. You're lettin' them push you off your game. You can't skate through them, you gotta find the open ice. Look for any opportunity you can get.

> *(They head back onto the ice,* **HELEN** *looks to the stands.)*

HELEN. Where the heck is Whippet?

> *(Whistle: Period two.)*

FOSTER HEWITT. Second period. Penalties adding up for both teams now. The game still scoreless. The Rivulettes using their speed. Oo! Helen Schmuck is down, hit by the stick of Winnipeg's Fran Grier.

HELEN. Learn how to hold a stick!

FOSTER HEWITT. Ranscombe has dropped her stick, and is exchanging punches with Winnipeg Forward Yvette Lambert.

FACH. Put your fists away ladies!

FOSTER HEWITT. The refs tear them apart, and they'll both go to the penalty box for that.

> *(Whistle:* **HILDA** *in the penalty box.)*

FACH. Too many penalties! Behave yourselves! Your moms are watching!

> *(Whistle: Game back on.)*

FOSTER HEWITT. Marm Schmuck passes the puck to Helen Schmuck. Ranscombe out of the box. Schmuck shoots! Off the post! And the rebound goes –

HILDA. Agh!

(**HILDA** *goes down on the ice hard.*)

MARM. Whoa!

ANNOUNCER. Lambert with the high hit! Ranscombe is down!

(*Whistle: Second intermission.*)

FACH. Come on Ref! What was that?!!

HILDA. I'm fine!

(*Spits out a tooth.*)

Have a tooth.

FACH. Here, let me see?

MARM. What more do we gotta do out there?

NELLIE. We're getting trapped in our own end.

FACH. (*Looking in* **HILDA**'s *mouth.*) We'll stitch it up later.

HELEN. Their goalie's stopping everything.

HILDA. If we lose this –

FACH. One goal! That's the only thing that matters right now. Not the Olympics, not Europe. One goal, ladies. Let's go!

(*Whistle: Period three.*)

NELLIE. (*Big save.*) Hah!

FOSTER HEWITT. The Eatons in the Rivulettes' end.

FACH. Come on Nellie!

FOSTER HEWITT. Throwing everything they have at Nellie Ranscombe –

FACH. Keep on them!

FOSTER HEWITT. But she's not having it.

FACH.	**FOSTER HEWITT.**
See the puck.	Johnson winds up! Saved by Ranscombe!

FACH. Good Ranscombe!! Now come on!

FOSTER HEWITT. Both goalies, owning the ice tonight folks. This is hockey at its finest. Unbelievable at both ends of the ice. It's a game of who's going to miss first.

FACH. Let's go! Let's go! Let's go now!

FOSTER HEWITT. Dying seconds of the third. It looks like we might be headed to overtime unless – Helen Schmuck with the puck, to Marm Schmuck, back to her sister –

FACH. Come on ladies! Control the puck! Let's get outta there!

FOSTER HEWITT. Winnipeg holding them in the Preston end. Marm Schmuck behind the net, to Ranscombe at the line – Whoa! On the breakaway!

FACH. Skate Ranscombe!! You got room! You got room! Shoot!

FOSTER HEWITT. She shoots!

HILDA. ...

FOSTER HEWITT. *She scores!!*

*(Whistle: **HILDA** scores. Game over.)*

FACH. Yahhhhhh!

HILDA.	**MARM.**
Ahhhh!!	Ahhhh!!

HELEN.	**NELLIE.**
Ahhhh!!!!	Aahhhh!!

(**HILDA** *falls to the ice and* **HELEN, NELLIE,** *and* **MARM** *embrace, jumping up and down, and pile on top of her.*)

FOSTER HEWITT. The time has run out for the Winnipeg Eatons! One-nothing Preston! The skilled lady hickory manipulators of Preston, are finally your National Champions! And the fans are on their feet!

Scene Twenty-Two
The Dance

(The celebratory win turns into a dance. Music plays on the radio. There's champagne. **FACH** drinks a beer and stands to the side by the radio. They are ecstatic, overflowing with excitement.)*

HELEN. You're definitely one of the girls now, Fach! Whether you like it or not!

NELLIE. When we're in Europe, I was thinking I could try a few games playing forward?

HILDA. Are you kidding?

NELLIE. Just to try it?

HELEN. After that performance, don't even think about leaving that net.

NELLIE. I wanna know what it feels like to score a goal.

HILDA. Then do it from our end of the ice.

MARM. We shut that department store down!

HELEN. Forget Whippet! I'm dancing with the best goalie in Canada!

HILDA. Girls'll be playing hockey all over the world!

MARM. In places where they've never even heard of it before! Where they don't even have ice!

HILDA. Where they've never even heard of ice.

MARM. Let me see your mouth?

---

*A license to produce *Glory* does not include a performance license for any third-party or copyrighted music. Licensees should create an original composition or use music in the public domain. For further information, please see Music and Third-Party Materials Use Note on page iii.

HILDA. I don't need it. Uh, the pain feels so good! I may be a sore winner, but I'm a much sorer loser.

> (**MARM** *holds the cold champagne bottle against* **HILDA**'s *face.*)

MARM. Hillbilly, you're a terrible loser.

HILDA. Thank you!

MARM. Coach Pocket! You gonna dance?

FACH. No.

HELEN. Come on Coach!

NELLIE.	HILDA.
One dance!	Just one!

MARM. Not even with a NATIONAL CHAMPION?!!

FACH. One dance. With a National Champion.

WOMEN. *(Laughing.)* Woo!!

RADIO CBC. We interrupt this broadcast to bring you the following announcement from our international partners at the BBC...

> (*A BBC Announcer translates in English over top of this section from Hitler's speech from September 1, 1939.*)

BBC ANNOUNCER.* "For the first time last night, Polish military invaded our territory and attacked from our soil. We have now been returning fire since 5:45 a.m.! And from now on, we shall repay bomb for bomb! There shall be no sacrifice in Germany that I would not take upon myself immediately... As a National Socialist and German soldier, I go into this battle with a strong heart! My whole life was but one continuous struggle for our people, for our resurrection, for Germany."

---

*Licensees will need to source these BBC recordings independently.

RADIO CBC. It is official. A declaration of war has been made by the German Führer, Adolf Hitler. Germany and Poland are now at war.

(**FACH** *turns off the radio.*)

HELEN. ...What does that mean?

FACH. ...

HELEN. Coach? What does that mean?

FACH. Another war.

NELLIE. He said Poland –

HILDA. And Germany not –

FACH. Britain and France will follow.

HELEN. And Canada.

FACH. ...

HELEN. He knows... I have to go.

NELLIE. I'll go with you.

HELEN. No, stay.

(*Taking them all in.*) I'm so happy we won.

(**HELEN** *leaves... A moment.*)

NELLIE. We're not going now are we?

HILDA. What?

MARM. We can't.

FACH. No.

HILDA. We'll go later though. Once it's over, once it's – We'll just keep playing until – And what about –

FACH. Hilda. It's bigger than that.

HILDA. I get that, but –

FACH. It's gonna change – the country – the – Everything. Teams were folding before...

NELLIE. You think we should fold too.

HILDA. We can't fold! I'll play one game a season if it means not folding. To hold on 'til it's all over.

FACH. We won the Dominion title. Whatever else happens at least we go out on top.

HILDA. I don't want to go out at all! We're the best in the country! We proved it! Just like you told us to. We proved it!

FACH. I'm sorry.

HILDA. ...You know, one day there's gonna be too many teams to play. And not just in this country, every country. And the refs will be women. The coaches. The managers. Because that's how long we've been playing. And there's not just a Dominion Championship, there's a World Championship! We're that good. And we go to the Olympics, and we win. Not because it's easy. Because we know how to play hard. Because we've waited for that moment our entire life. My life can be about playing hockey all the time, if I choose. And I've stopped thinking, that no matter how many times we win...I'm still going to lose.

(**HILDA** *leaves.*)

FACH. ...You know... The only reason Homuth gave you the money was to get back at me? ...We were both just kids but I took him into the boards pretty bad... He didn't walk for six months. Neither of us played again. He thought he coulda been the next Cyclone Taylor. Me too... Me, coachin' women's hockey was some sorta... But this country's got plenty of boys dreamin' about hockey. We need you.

We got an exhibition game in Woodstock next month against the Hamilton Tigers. If we can get Woodstock to form a team then – And the Ottawa Rangers are still in.

NELLIE. I should go see if –

MARM. Yeah.

NELLIE. Thanks, Coach.

MARM. Yeah, thanks.

(**MARM** *and* **NELLIE** *leave.* **FACH** *is left alone.*)

Scene Twenty-Three
We Play to Win

(A month later... **MARM, HELEN,** *and* **NELLIE** *are in the locker room, half-dressed.)*

MARM. Sixteen thousand women! From all over the country. That's how many they're hiring.

HELEN. And you'd rather do that than make shoes?

MARM. Fifty pairs a week!!

HELEN. Right.

MARM. And I'd be helping with the war effort.

NELLIE. How is sixteen thousand women making guns helping anything?

MARM. Isn't it better to have more on our side than theirs?

HELEN. Can we just...

MARM. Sorry. But they're giving people jobs and –

      *(***HILDA** *enters.)*

Hilda even applied.

NELLIE. You did?

HILDA. I thought I'd give it a try.

MARM. How hard can it be? I mean, we've won the Dominion Championship so everything else is gonna seem –

HELEN. I'm pregnant... That's supposed to be good news, isn't it?

HILDA. It is good news.

NELLIE. It's great news.

MARM. I told you.

NELLIE. So, shouldn't you...?

HELEN. It's just an exhibition game. No hitting right? And no slap shots! Besides, it could be our –

MARM. Don't say it!

HELEN. But it's true. This could be the last game we ever play together.

NELLIE. What are we even doing here?

HILDA. Playing the Tigers.

HELEN. Ten more teams have folded.

NELLIE. There's nothing left to play for, Hill.

HILDA. We play to win.

NELLIE. We've already lost.

HILDA. We have not! We'll play together again, I know we will. I'm not afraid of that. We're far too determined! Too competitive! It may take longer than I want it to. We might have to start all over again. But instead of feeling sorry for ourselves, instead of feeling angry, can't we be proud? Of what we did? Can't we go out there and remember how good it feels to just play?

> (**HILDA** *picks up her jersey and begins to get dressed, as do they all.* **MARM** *quietly begins to sing.* **HILDA, HELEN,** *and* **NELLIE** *join her.*)

MARM.

OH CANADA. OUR HOME AND NATIVE LAND. TRUE PATRIOT LOVE

MARM & HILDA.

THOU DOST IN US COMMAND.

MARM, HILDA, HELEN & NELLIE.

WITH GLOWING HEARTS WE SEE THEE RISE, THE TRUE NORTH STRONG AND FREE.

AND STAND ON GUARD, O CANADA, WE STAND ON GUARD
FOR THEE.

(They stand in a line at center ice. Warming up, focused. **FACH** *stands up behind the boards and joins them.)*

ALL.

OH CANADA, GLORIOUS AND FREE!
WE STAND ON GUARD, WE STAND ON GUARD FOR THEE.

(Through them we are reminded of the Nagano Olympics in 1998, the 2002 Olympics in Salt Lake City where the Canadians first won gold, and what is still to come.)

O CANADA, WE STAND ON GUARD FOR THEE.

(They push off as the lights fade to black.)

End of Play

Preston Springs Rivulettes

*The premiere production used the first 17 bars, if you'd like to shorten it.

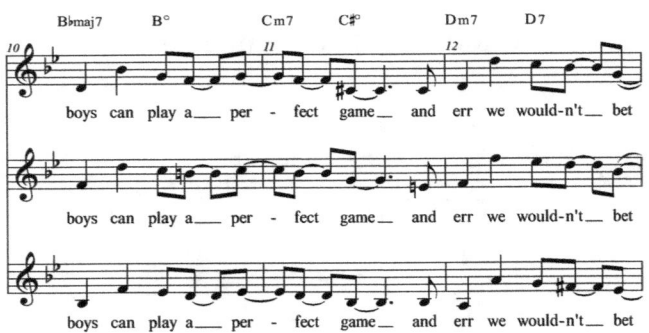

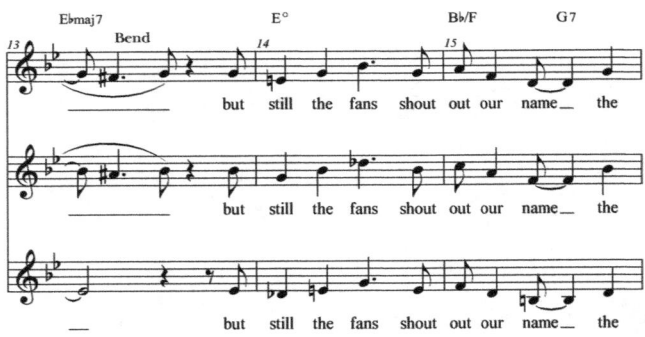

Preston Springs Rivulettes - p.4